SELF-SERVE MURDER

DEATH BY CUPCAKE, BOOK #3

D.E. HAGGERTY

Also by D.E. Haggerty

Dedication

To all the readers who have to hide in the bathroom to finish 'just one more chapter' because their spouse just won't shut up.

P.S. Love you, babe

Chapter 1

Insert coffee to begin

I groan and roll over. Try to roll over is more like it. For some reason, my body is not following my mind's commands. Not that my mind is totally with it either. It feels fuzzy, or maybe, like I'm under water or something. I take a few deep breaths before trying the whole roll-over in bed thing again. I can do this. I've been rolling over on my own in bed for nearly twenty-three years. I got this.

Except, I don't. I grunt before giving it one more college try. I gather all my energy and push my body to turn so that I can get out of this bed. And I need to get out. My bladder has decided the time to move was like five minutes ago. I manage to move ever so slightly only to run into something. Did I fall asleep with my study books again? I manage to unglue my eyes and turn my head to the side. *Who in the name of caramel mocha lattes is that?*

My eyes nearly pop out of my head. Why in the world is there a man in my bed? "Hey dude." My voice sounds like sandpaper scratched my vocal cords. I clear my throat and try again. "Dude! Wake up! What are you doing here?" He doesn't respond, so I reach out and push his shoulder. Ugh! He's not wearing a shirt and his skin is clammy. I reach down to wipe my hand on my night shirt, but it's not there. I look down at myself and nearly come out of my skin.

Holy hot coffee! I'm naked as the day I was born. *Stay calm. Stay calm.* There must be a reasonable explanation for my being naked in bed with a man I don't know and not remembering a single little thing about it. Oh

5

my goodness, that sounds bad. Real bad. Maybe dude knows what's going on.

I turn back to mystery man. "Dude! Wake up!" I don't make the mistake of touching his clammy shoulder again because eww, just eww. Instead, I poke him in his side. Uh oh. Even with only touching him with my finger, I can feel more clammy skin. I don't want to look, but I have to. I take a breath to steel myself against what I'll find before allowing my eyes to move from his face down his body.

Oh. My. God. Not only is there a man in my bed I don't know, but he's passed out. And he's naked. I've never even seen a naked man before. Well, not up close and personal. And he's lying on his back with his junk hanging out. Not that I'm looking. Okay, I'm looking. Is that what a man's junk looks like? That's not attractive at all. It's wrinkly and small. Way smaller than I expected.

I shake my head and look away. This is totally not the way I thought my first experience with a naked man in my bed would be like. Not. At. All. I'm not sure if I want to wake him or just sneak out and hope he's not here when I get back. Wow. That's completely cowardly lion territory. I am not the cowardly lion. I am the fierce lioness. I can do this.

"Dude!" I shout as loud as my scratchy throat will allow me. "Wake. Up. Now!" He doesn't move at all. What the heck is up with this guy?

Uh oh. Clammy skin. I may not be a doctor, but I am a doctor's daughter who was forced to take first aid, CPR, and every other remotely medical class offered by the Red Cross in my hometown. With shaking hands, I reach over and put my fingers to his neck checking for a pulse. I wait for the ba-bum ba-bum rhythm. I feel nothing. That can't be right. I must be doing something wrong. I reach out and grab his hand; immediately putting my fingers to the inside of his wrist. Nothing.

I scream and start scrambling over him to get out of the bed. My foot gets caught on something – I'm not even going to consider what that 'something' could be –

Self-Serve Murder

and I trip landing on my butt on the floor. I crab walk away from the naked man on my bed as fast as my shaky limbs will allow. My movement ends when I hit something solid. I put my back to the wall, draw my knees into my chest, wrap my arms around them, and try to get myself under control. This can't be happening. I must be dreaming. Stuff like this doesn't happen to me. I'm the good girl. The boring girl. I'm still a virgin for gosh sakes! At twenty-three!

I must be dreaming. That's the only plausible explanation to this scenario. I reach down and pinch my side as hard as I can. Darn it! That hurt. Which means this is not a dream. Okay, Kristie, get yourself together. You can do this. You work at a youth center frequented by gang members. You have no fear. No. Fear.

I stand on wobbly legs and move to the door where I grab the robe hanging from a hook on the back of it. I quickly cover myself before approaching the man again. I need to help him. If he isn't dead, that is. I lay my head on his chest. Nothing happens. No movement whatsoever. I check again for a pulse even though my mind has already come to a gruesome conclusion. He's gone.

I grab my phone and hit speed dial.

"Good morning, Sunshine!" The voice on the other end is entirely too chipper.

"I need help." I can barely get the words out.

Anna doesn't hesitate. "Where are you?"

"Home," I answer before disconnecting the call. Anna will come. The pink-haired pixie will know what to do.

✦✦✦

The rumble of the words 'stay here' brings me out of my stupor. I have no idea how much time has passed since I crawled back into the corner. I take a deep breath and try to stand, but I don't manage to move before the door is flung open and a man bursts in, gun raised. I immediately shrink back into the corner and make myself as small as possible.

"Logan! You're scaring the frosting out of her!" A familiar voice shouts before hands reach for me. Her hands are everywhere, touching and inspecting me. I finally gain control of my voice when she starts to open my robe. "Hey!" My scratchy voice stuns Anna enough that I'm able to bat her hands away. I push her aside and manage to stand.

I tower over her when I stand. Her five-feet height is no barrier to my seeing the entourage, which she apparently brought with her. Behind Anna, her boyfriend, Logan, and my boss's boyfriend, Ben, are standing over the body. And immediately behind Anna hovers my boss, Callie. Callie owns the bakery *Callie's Cakes* where I work as a barista and Anna as the baker phenomenon.

Logan and Ben are both cops. As I watch them, Logan reaches over and checks naked dude's pulse. He pulls away and shakes his head. Ben whips out his phone and walks out of my overcrowded bedroom. I panic when I realize that he's a police officer and probably calling into the desk or whatever policemen do when they discover a crime.

"No!" I shout before trying to chase after him. Anna squeaks as I easily mow her down, but Callie's not as easily ignored. She may be two inches shorter than me at five-feet-five-inches, but she's got sexy curves that go on for days and she's not afraid to use them. She wraps me in a hug and refuses to let go as I struggle with her.

"Shh," she whispers into my ear. "It's okay. You're okay."

I start to growl before I can stop myself. I don't growl. I'm the good girl. I take a deep breath in through my nose before letting it out of my mouth. "I know, I'm okay. I don't know, however, if I'm a murderer. I'd prefer to figure that out before the cops arrive." I somehow manage to speak in a normal voice, the scratchiness slowly disappearing the more I exercise my vocal cords.

Anna barks out a laugh behind me. "Seriously? How in the world can you possibly think you're a killer?" She snorts. "You're Ms. I'm-gonna-save-the-world."

Self-Serve Murder

I roll my eyes at her assessment of me. She doesn't know me as well as she thinks she does. Callie still has her arms around me and she pushes me into the desk chair across from my bed. "Kristie," she says as she kneels on the floor in front of the chair. "Can you tell us what happened?"

I shake my head. "I have no idea. I woke up ..." I pause as I feel my cheeks heat up. I lean forward and whisper, "... naked." I clear my throat after that embarrassing admission before continuing. "This dude was in my bed with me."

"Do you have any idea who he is?" Anna asks from the position she took up next to Callie.

I continue to shake my head. "No idea. I've never seen him before."

"What's the last thing you remember?" Before I get a chance to answer Callie's question, I hear sirens. My heart starts to pound. What if they're here to arrest me? I rub my hand over my pounding heart and stare wide-eyed at Callie.

Logan grabs Anna and lifts her out of her place. He gives Callie a look I can't interpret but which causes my boss woman to back away as well. When they've retreated, Logan gets on his knees in front of me. He looks briefly at the floor before looking me into the eyes and speaking. "Kristie, sweetheart, do you remember how you got home?"

The sirens are getting closer. I have no idea how I got home, let alone how I ended up in bed with a man I don't know. And now the police are coming to get me! I try to stand, but Logan grabs my hands.

"Sweetheart, is there any reason you'd be naked in bed with a man you don't know?"

My eyes nearly pop out of my head. Is that his way of asking me if I do one-night stands? I shake my head vigorously but that causes my head to ache and my stomach to roll. "Kristie, we need you to go to the hospital." He says and leans over me. I panic and try to escape, but

I'm stuck in my chair. Anna immediately rushes over.

"It's okay, Logan would never hurt you," she whispers and turns to nod at the man himself to proceed.

"I'm going to pick you up now. I'm going to carry you to my car and we're going to go to the hospital. Is that okay?" I just stare at him. Anna reaches forward and grabs my hand.

"I'll be with you the whole time," she says as she squeezes my hand. "I won't leave you alone with anyone. And you know, no one's getting through me." The tiny pixie's bravado makes a ghost of a smile appear on my face and I nod.

Logan picks me up as the paramedics rush through the door. He nods at them and points with his chin at my bed. Callie's standing in the living room as we exit my bedroom. She grabs my free hand and tries to smile at me. "I'm going to pack you a bag, okay?" She doesn't wait for my response and rushes into my bedroom after the paramedics.

Logan carries me to his car with Anna holding my hand the entire way. She scoots into the back seat before her boyfriend lowers me onto the seat next to her. He shuts the door gently behind him before getting into the driver's seat to drive us to the hospital. I stare out of the window and try to remember last night, but my memories are fuzzy. I know I went to the college bar down the street but, everything after I took the first sips of my beer, is a blur.

Chapter 2

Coffeeology: Take life one cup at a time

We drive up to the emergency room entrance and Logan dashes out of the car to grab a wheelchair. He lifts me gently into the chair and wheels it inside while Anna walks beside me squeezing my hand. Police must get better treatment at the ER than normal folk, because we're immediately ushered into a private examination room. A real examination room with a door and everything. Even though my dad is a plastic surgeon, he does spend some time in emergency rooms and I've been with him when he's been called in for an emergency a few times. An actual room with walls and such is a luxury I've never seen.

"Miss," the doctor says when he arrives while looking pointedly at Anna. "You're going to have to leave."

Anna squares her shoulders and heads off with the man. "I'm not leaving Kristie alone after what happened." She turns to Logan. "They can't make me, can they?"

Logan's eyes soften as he smiles at her and shakes his head. When he turns to the doctor, he's back to scary-as-all-get-out cop. "She's staying." His voice has me nearly shaking in my boots – if I had boots on – and he's not even talking to me. The doctor seems to agree with my assessment and just nods.

"I'll be right outside this door," Logan says as he tilts his head to the hallway. "If you need anything, just shout. Or tell Anna and she'll take care of it." The corners of his mouth quirk up at that before he turns and leaves.

A nurse rushes in as Logan closes the door. After the nurse removes my robe, the doctor does a quick physical exam before taking several samples of blood. As soon as the needle leaves my body, Anna is helping me pull the thin excuse for a blanket over my body.

The doctor clears his throat and sits on the rolling stool next to me. He looks me right in the eyes and asks. "Do we need to do a rape kit?"

My eyes nearly bug out of my head. Despite waking up naked next to a dead man who was also naked, it never occurred to me that I may have been violated in that way. "I don't think so." My voice is trembling as I answer. "I've never you know…" My voice trails off as my face explodes in heat.

"Shall I just take a look to make sure everything is still intact?" The doctor forms the words as a question, but he's already moving around to the end of the bed and giving the nurse instructions with his eyes.

The nurse slides the curtain in front of the door to give us complete privacy. Logan's face turns hard as he disappears from my sight. Anna grabs my hand and squeezes with all her might. "Just look at me, sweet cheeks. This will be over in less time than it takes me to frost a cupcake."

Fortunately, she's right. Before I have a chance to contemplate why a bed in the ER has stirrups, the doctor is rolling his stool away from me and snapping his gloves off. He nods at the nurse and she grabs a gown, which Anna insists on helping me into. As soon as I'm covered, the nurse moves the curtain away from the door and Logan barges in.

The doctor ignores him as he stands and moves to the sink in the corner to wash his hands. "Everything looks normal."

"So I wasn't…" I can't seem to finish a sentence today.

He smiles at me gently and shakes his head. "No."

"Thank god," Logan mumbles as his body visibly relaxes. He stands behind Anna before reaching out and squeezing my shoulder.

The doctor finishes with the sink and grabs my chart. "Based on your symptoms, memory loss, confusion, drowsiness, it looks like you were given Rohypnol. We'll know for sure when the lab results are back." That's as far as he gets before Anna explodes.

"She was given the date rape drug! How could this happen?"

Logan hugs her to him and shushes her. "Let the doc talk."

The doctor clears his throat and continues. "You should be completely fine in a few hours. Drink plenty of liquids, get some rest." He gives me another gentle smile before looking at Logan. "I assume you want a report?" Logan nods in response.

The doctor closes his clipboard. "Take all the time you need," he says before quietly leaving.

"What..." Anna's question is cut off by Logan.

"Can you tell us the last thing you remember?"

I shake my head and stare at the door. "I went to Dylan's, the bar just down the street from my place. I had one beer." I stop. I don't remember anything after that. I shake my head. "Sorry."

Logan reaches over and squeezes my hand. "Don't worry about it."

Ben and Callie rush in before he can continue. Or at least Callie rushes in. Ben just saunters in behind her. She smiles at me before handing me my backpack. I quickly unzip it to find a pair of jeans and sweater. "Thanks," I mumble as I root around looking for some underwear.

"I've got your coat and a pair of boots as well." She holds up the items and I nod in appreciation.

Ben and Logan move to the corner of the room and start whispering.

13

"Oh, no you don't," Anna shouts as she crosses her arms. "You're not going all secret-spy cops on us now. Kristie deserves to know what's going on."

I roll my eyes at her before turning to the guys. "Yeah, a heads-up before I get arrested for murder might be nice." Callie and Anna, who have both spent time at the police station getting grilled for murders they obviously didn't commit, join in on my protestations. The men don't stand a chance.

Ben rolls his eyes and throws his arms in the air. "We're not trying to keep things from Kristie. And she's definitely not being arrested for murder."

The tightness in my chest releases as I digest those words. "I'm not? Really?"

Ben approaches the bed. "No, sweetie, you're not." He smiles at me and I can understand why Callie melts every time the man is near. He's absolutely gorgeous when he aims that smile at you.

"Do you know who the dead dude was?" Now that I'm not going to be immediately arrested for murder, I need to know who I woke up with. Someone out there has lost a loved one and they don't even know it yet. That situation needs to be rectified, stat. Ben shakes his head in response to my question, but he doesn't get a chance to speak before my name is shouted.

"Kristie? What are you doing here?"

I take a deep breath and plaster on the biggest smile I can muster before turning my head to the voice. "Hi, Mr. Timmer. What are *you* doing here?" I cringe when I hear how sharp my voice sounds.

He waves a hand in dismissal of my question. "Just visiting a friend."

I blink my eyes in surprise at the unexpected guest. Mr. Timmer is my graduate counselor at the School of Social Work at the university where I'm working on my Master's in Social Work. He's a sweet guy and super supportive of my career, but I don't want everyone on campus to know what happened to me. Before I have a chance to think of a believable lie as to why I'm here, Logan speaks.

"Who's your friend, Kristie?" The sentence is formed like a question, but Logan's voice makes it clear that he expects an answer. I nearly roll my eyes at him being all protective. The man may be hot as Hades and super sweet to Anna, but he still scares the daylights out of me.

"This is Mr. Timmer. He's my academic advisor in the social work program." I nod to Callie. "That's Professor Muller from the German department and also my boss."

Callie stretches out a hand to Timmer. He reluctantly lets me go to shake her hand. "I don't think we've met before. Nice to meet you," she says with a smile. Ben wraps his arms around her and practically yanks her away from my advisor. Now I do roll my eyes. These men take being protective to the nth degree.

"I work with Anna." I point to the pink-haired pixie. "Ben and Logan are their boyfriends."

Mr. Timmer barely glances at the men before turning back to me and grabbing my hand again. "Are you okay? What happened?" His eyes roam over my body as if he's looking for some type of injury, but they stop on my breasts. I follow his gaze and notice the blanket has fallen away and my breasts are nearly visible through the just-not-see-through gown. I quickly grab the blanket with my free hand and pull it to my chin.

"I'm fine." I wouldn't tell him what happened for all the coffee in the world. I wiggle my hand until he releases me. He may be a sweet guy who's supportive of my career but that doesn't mean I want him touching me. He's my advisor for coffee's sake.

Mr. Timmer obviously feels the chilliness that has descended on the room upon his arrival. "Well, okay then. I guess I'll be heading out. I'll see you at school," he announces before scurrying from the room without saying a word to anyone else.

"Is it me or was that guy weird?" Anna doesn't

even wait for the door to shut behind him before she opens her mouth.

I shake my head at her. "Give him a break. He had some kind of breakdown or something in his previous job so he does advising now." I shiver as I recall his fascination with my womanly assets. "But that was kind of creepy."

"Total creepsville." She nods in agreement before loudly announcing, "Let's blow this popsicle stand."

Chapter 3

I'm pretty sure BC actually stands for 'Before Coffee'

I assumed that as soon as we got back to my apartment, everyone would take off and I'd be left alone to contemplate what happened. Contemplate. I snort to myself. Freak out's more like it. Unfortunately, when I open the door and turn around to thank everyone, the men push their way in before sauntering over to my sofa and collapsing on it. My sofa, heck my apartment, was not made to house the two oversized detectives.

I don't shut the door but stand at the entrance with my mouth opening and closing in my best imitation of a fish. *Think, think, think.* Oh yeah, I have the perfect excuse for keeping them out. "Should you be in here? Doesn't CSI or whatever it's called in real life need to do their thing? Find clues or fingerprints or something?" There! That sounded reasonable. Not at all like I'm trying to kick everyone out.

Logan snorts. "You watch too much TV."

Luckily, Ben takes pity on me and explains. "They've already come and gone. And even if they hadn't, it wouldn't matter." The confusion must show on my face. The big detective smiles. "We were all here this morning." *Duh.* I nod my head in understanding but don't move away from the door.

Anna sits on Logan's lap and I cringe as my sofa creaks. "You might as well shut the door and come in here." Oh great, the troublemaker is on the case. Looks like I don't have a choice. I shut the door and walk the short distance to my living room. I collapse in the chair across from my friends and close my eyes. Let the questions begin.

"So why were you in that bar anyway? You don't drink. Or at least the few times we've gone out, we nearly had to force-feed you beer." Callie's voice sounds genuinely hurt.

I shrug and try to evade giving away the real reason for my visit to the bar. "Am I not allowed to go to a bar on a Friday night?"

"That's not what I meant and you know it," Callie immediately snaps. Darn it! I suck at the secret spy mission stuff.

"Sorry, I'm not feeling well." There, that's not a lie.

"We just need you to answer a few questions and then we'll leave you alone," Ben insists in a gentle but firm voice. Obviously, I'm not getting out of answering some questions and considering I woke up naked next to a dead man, I should probably be grateful I'm getting grilled by my friends instead of cuddling up to some jailbird named Bertha.

"What do you want to know?" My voice may sound a bit whiney, but I'm not about to reveal my secret. An offense is the best defense or something like that, right?

"What do you remember about last night? What time did you go to the bar?" Ben's the one asking questions, but the others are paying close attention, watching me with sharp eyes. I lean back and close my eyes again. Maybe if I can't see my friends, I can pretend I'm not lying to their faces.

I shrug. "I guess it was about nine or so when I walked over there."

"Did you have anything to drink?"

"Just a beer. Not enough to get me drunk or anything."

"Did you open the bottle yourself?"

I snort. Of course, I didn't drink from a bottle. "I had a draft. Friday is fifty-cent draft night."

"So, basically anyone could have tampered with your drink?"

I nod. I figured that out a while ago.

"But why? It doesn't make any sense. You were given the date-rape drug, but you weren't ..." Callie clears her throat before skipping over the word everyone is thinking. "Why would someone give you a drug? And then there's the whole dead guy thing. Why did someone put a dead guy in bed with you? It's almost like someone's framing you. But why would someone frame you? You're the good girl. You never get in trouble." My face heats up as Callie gets closer and closer to the truth. Luckily, Anna slaps her best friend and she finally stops rambling and yelps, "Sorry."

"It's okay." I open my eyes to smile at Callie. Unfortunately, the men are studying me and my face and neck feel the heat – literally. I can't look them in the eyes.

"What's going on?" Anna asks as she raises an eyebrow in question at her boyfriend whose stare is way too perceptive. She looks from him to me and back again. "Why are you blushing?" Naturally, her words make me blush even more. "Holy cupcakes! There is a reason you would be targeted!"

"What? No!" I shake my head but avoid looking at her.

"Look me in the eyes and tell me you haven't been up to anything," Anna demands.

"Oh for coffee's sake," I mutter.

"Spill it!"

I cross my arms over my chest and try to downplay my actions. "There's just this thing I've been looking into. It's no big deal."

Anna snorts. "No big deal. That's why you ended up drugged lying next to a dead man."

"Anna!" It's now Callie's turn to slap her best friend. "Be nice."

The tiny troublemaker shrugs. "She's hiding

something." She turns to me. "What's going on, Kristie?"

Bugger. "I'm sure it's not the reason I was targeted," I hedge, still unwilling to give up my secret.

Callie gasps. "Oh my god, Anna was right! You're hiding something." She stares at me a moment and it's almost like I can actually see a light bulb go off above her head. She smirks and relaxes against Ben. "That explains everything."

"Explains everything?" Anna huffs in frustration.

Callie rolls her eyes at her best friend. "You know," she sweeps her arm out at me. "Kristie's been totally acting weird and out of character for a few months now."

The fairy baker turns on me. "You got some 'splaining to do, girl."

I sigh and close my eyes. Confessions should never be done in the harsh light of daytime. "I may have been doing some digging around into a mystery of my own." I hear the indignant gasps from Anna and Callie and nearly smile. Those two think they're some great detectives out of an Agatha Christie novel or something just because they solved the mystery of who murdered Callie's pole-dancing instructor; a crime which Callie was accused of committing. And then Anna's friend went and got murdered and they solved that mystery as well. I haven't been as lucky with my crime solving adventures.

"Several undergrads in the social worker program have been raped. All with the same MO; drugged and woke up back in their dorm not remembering what happened but having been violated."

Now it's the men's turn to explode. "And you didn't think to tell us this earlier?" Logan accuses. I open my eyes to find him and Ben standing in front of my chair; vibrating with anger.

"I wasn't raped." They shake their heads in response. "And I woke up with a dead guy in my bed. That's totally not the rapist's MO."

Ben kneels in front of my chair and grabs my hands. "Sweetheart, that's exactly why you should have told us. This could be a message from the perp – don't mess with me or else."

Logan is standing immediately behind Ben with his arms crossed over his chest. "Have you been asking questions down at the Youth Center?" The Youth Center is where I work as part of my field placement requirements in the Master of Social Work program. I received my Bachelor's in Social Work in the Spring and started on my master's a few months ago. The center is a sort of gathering place slash safe house for pre-teens and teenagers who are at risk of joining gangs.

I shrug in response to Logan's question. "Not really. Just keeping my eyes and ears open."

Logan shoves his hands through his hair in obvious frustration. He works in the gang division at the police department but before that, he was undercover in a gang for years. If anyone has intimate knowledge of what the local gangs are capable of, it's him. He turns on Anna. "You are not to go running around the Youth Center looking for clues and trying to solve this."

Anna widens her eyes in innocence. "Of course not." She shakes her head. "That'd be dangerous."

"You either," Ben demands of Callie.

She actually dares to roll her eyes at the man. "Whatever."

"Sweetheart," he says in a soft voice and I can literally see her melt. She nods and mumbles something to him.

And then the two police officers, their faces like thunder, rush out of my apartment. I stare at the door and wonder what in the world just happened.

Chapter 4

OCD: Obsessive Coffee Disorder

The door is barely closed behind the men before Anna rubs her hands in glee and announces. "Okay! How are we going to find this bad guy?"

My eyes nearly bug out of my head. "What? You just promised Logan you wouldn't do any snooping around."

Anna shakes her head and smirks at me. "Nope! I promised I wouldn't do any snooping around at the Youth Center." She shrugs. "I may or may not live up to that promise. In the meantime, however, we need to start our own investigation."

I look to Callie for help in reigning in the lunatic, but she's nodding in agreement. "I don't think the rapes were committed by a gang member. It's too thought out and clinical for them. I'm not an expert, but from what I understand, these gang members get off on violence. A drugged woman wouldn't put up a fight."

I shiver as the implication of her words moves through me. That could have been me last night.

"Before we get started on our plan of action, I need some answers," Anna announces.

Uh oh. I nearly don't dare to ask. "Answers about what?"

The pink-haired sprite throws her hands up in the air. "How in the world are you still a virgin?" I gulp. This is not a conversation I want to have. Anna completely ignores my uneasiness. "I mean – look at you." She waves a hand up and down my body. "You're freaking gorgeous. You are *the* girl-next-door that every football quarterback wants to have on his arm and definitely in his bed. Long blonde hair, blue eyes, a perfect hourglass figure. What's up?"

To my utter embarrassment, I can feel my face flaming. Callie tries to save me. "Anna, if she doesn't want to talk about this, it's none of our business."

Anna huffs and crosses her arms over her chest before collapsing on the sofa. "Fine. But I thought we were besties. Besties tell each other this kind of stuff."

Gosh darned it. I don't want to talk about this, but maybe she's right. This is something besties would talk about. Fine. I'll tell them. Decision made, I square my shoulders and stare at Anna. She looks eager and excited. I can't help but shake my head at the high-strung pixie. "It's not really a big deal. The boys in high school only wanted to date me because of my father." Anna snorts, but I ignore her. "They would come over and be all *Dr. Larson, whose nose did you fix today? Was she famous?*"

"I'm sure not all the boys wanted to date you just because your father was a well-known plastic surgeon," Callie disagrees in a gentle voice.

"There's more." I swallow before I continue. "Turns out there was a whole gambling pool of who would take my virginity."

"No!" Anna shouts and jumps up from the sofa. "I'll go kick their butts!" She does some boxing moves and what I think are supposed to be kicks.

I can't help but laugh at the tiny tornado. "Good luck finding them. I'm not in high school anymore." I don't bother adding that I went to high school in another city.

"Oh yeah." She sounds disappointed as she collapses on the sofa.

Callie leans forward. "You haven't been in high school for years, Kristie. Are you saving yourself for marriage? There's nothing wrong with that." She nods as she starts to spout nerd. "Approximately five percent of women in the U.S. wait until they're married. It's actually kind of sweet."

I giggle as I shake my head. There's nothing sweet about my decision. "I'm not saving myself, but it's not like I exactly have time to date." Despite having a rich family, I pay for my tuition as well as room and board. Working two part-time jobs and going to school full-time doesn't exactly leave much time for a social life.

Anna claps her hands. "One thing at a time. We'll solve your little situation some other time. For now, we need to solve a murder."

I gulp. A murder. How could I have possibly forgotten that?

"We don't know it's murder yet," Callie reminds us. "We need to solve these rapes and protect the women of this campus. That's what's important. Even though I have a feeling whoever the rapist is, is the murderer as well. Assuming the man was murdered of course."

"What have you learned so far?" Anna's voice is now all business. These ladies sure take their crime solving seriously.

"Not much," I admit.

"Let's start at the beginning. How did you find out about the rapes?"

"Mostly rumors. I tried talking to the campus police, but they weren't exactly willing to discuss criminal investigations with a grad student."

Callie whips out a notebook and pen from her ever-present messenger bag. "So what do you know?"

I shrug. "Just what I said earlier – all the victims were roofied and woke up back at their dorm naked and assaulted."

"And all the victims are in the social worker program?"

I shake my head. "I'm not really sure. Those are the ones that I've heard about because I'm in the program.

There may be other victims I don't know about."

"What else do you know about the victims?" Anna asks as Callie scratches away in her notebook.

"That's kind of it."

Callie taps her pen on her notebook. "We need to know more about the victims. Establish a pattern. That way we can figure out how the victims are being targeted."

Anna snaps her fingers. "I've got it! There must be police reports or something. We can look through those."

She doesn't even finish talking before Callie's shaking her head. "Assuming all the rapes occurred on campus, the reports are protected by privacy regulations. We can't get our hands on them." Anna starts to open her mouth again, but Callie cuts her off. "And there's no way we're asking Ben or Logan to get them." She shrugs. "I don't think they could anyway."

It's quiet for a moment before Anna blurts out. "What about forums?"

"Forums?" I raise an eyebrow in confusion.

Anna shrugs. "When I was working for Arthur, he was always talking about the people he met online in forums." Arthur was a genius computer geek who Anna worked for before he got himself killed. Long story.

"That's not a bad idea." Callie shuts her notebook. "The university has an intranet and there's all kinds of groups and such on it."

I shake my head at her. "I doubt anyone's using the intranet to discuss something so... intimate."

"It's possible to set up private forums and chat rooms and the like." I just stare at her and wait for her to elaborate. She huffs. "It turns out students think my exams are difficult and there was this whole forum-thing with questions and answers from several years of exams. I guess that's pretty common."

After I calm my giggles from Callie's indignation, I think about the possibility. She could be right. I'm way too busy to spend my time chatting online or whatever it's called, but there are students who are continuously doing something or other online. I've always assumed they were on social media. Wait. Do forums fall under the guise of social media? I don't even know that much.

Anna and Callie stand. "Okay," Anna says as she comes over to pull me out of my chair for a hug. "We're going to let you get some rest. Call if you need anything."

Callie grabs my hand and squeezes. "Don't worry about work tomorrow. We'll take care of it."

I start to protest but change my mind. I can use the time I should be making coffees for the masses tomorrow to do some research into forums.

Chapter 5

Oh goodie! It's coffee o'clock!

Instead of getting dressed and heading off to *Callie's Cakes* on Sunday morning, I make myself a huge coffee and sit behind my laptop. I may not be much of a computer person, but after months of getting nowhere, I'm willing to try anything. It's obvious my methods – eavesdropping on conversations and going to bars to see if I can catch someone putting drugs in the drinks – are not working and may even be dangerous. Okay, it's dangerous. There, I admitted it. Just don't tell Callie or Anna. And definitely don't say anything to their hunky police boyfriends.

I haven't spent much time on the university intranet. I use it, somewhat against my will, for turning in assignments when required and checking my course grades, but otherwise, I don't really see the need for it. I may have been born in a time period when everyone seems to be surgically connected to electronic devices, but that doesn't automatically mean I am as well. I've got way too much energy to sit still behind a computer and when I'm out and about, I like to spend my time people watching. Oh – and I prefer to not walk into things because my eyes are glued to my phone.

I feel like a two-headed dinosaur as I search for a forum. It takes me an embarrassing amount of time before I even find any. It turns out there are absolutely tons of them. I scroll through a few, my eyes starting to glaze over, when I realize the forums are divided by college. I quickly go to my own college – the School of Social Work.

There. At least that narrows things down a bit. I spend another half-hour searching the various forums before stumbling upon this:

Unconscious does not equal unhurt – private group

I dance in my seat with excitement. After spending the past few months trying to find out what in the world is going on with this campus and getting absolutely nowhere, I may have finally found some information. I immediately click on the *request to join group* button. A message pops up: *This forum and associated chatrooms are private. Please indicate why you think you should have entry to this group.*

Huh. That's a bit mysterious. Nothing about the purpose or goals of the group. But the name of the group is like a flashing beacon. This is exactly how those women would feel – and rightfully so. I type in a message:

I'm searching for a support group after what happened to me on Friday night. Maybe your group can help?

I don't want to give too much away in case this group isn't what I'm looking for. I don't exactly want the entire campus knowing what happened. After waking up naked and not remembering anything that happened, I've been embarrassed enough for the rest of my life – thank you very much. I hit send and wait. There's a response in less than a minute.

This group is available by recommendation only.

Recommendation only? Why didn't you say so in the first place? Maybe this isn't the group I'm looking for after all. I immediately type back: *Sorry, I thought you might be able to help me.*

I'm surprised when I get a reply. *What do you think this group is for?*

Assuming my profile is private and the administrator can't figure out who I am, I respond: *For students who've been roofied.*

Did that happen to you?

Yes.

That must be the magic word because the forum suddenly opens up to me. I quickly confirm membership and make up a user name. Then, I spend some time navigating the various threads. I stumble upon the thread *Introduce Yourself* and start reading.

The first story is from Alex and it's a tearjerker. Alex was a freshman when she was roofied at a frat party. Just like me, she woke up naked in her own bed not remembering how she got there or what happened to her. Except something definitely did happen to her. It was obvious she had been sexually assaulted. She went to the free clinic on campus for medical assistance and they sent her to the campus police.

The campus police were useless. With no memory of what happened and no DNA, they had no evidence and apparently no clue on how to run an investigation. They took Alex's statement but made it perfectly clear that they weren't planning on doing anything with it. They claimed there wasn't anything they could do.

Alex tried to get back to normal, but she couldn't. She started having panic attacks and withdrew from everyone. She went home for Thanksgiving break but never returned to campus. She dropped out of college without even finishing her first semester. My heart breaks as I read her story. I wonder how she's doing now.

I see that Alex is online and send her a private message asking if she wants to chat. A private chat box immediately opens up.

Me: *Hi, I'm Kristie. I just read your story. If you don't mind me asking, how are you doing?*

Alex: *Just trying to survive one day at a time.*

Me: *Gosh. I hope the days get better as they go along.*

Alex ignores my admittedly lame attempt at support and instead asks: *Did something happen to you?*

Me: *I was roofied on Friday night.*

Alex: *Are you ok?*

Me: *Yeah, but I want to find the bastard.*

Alex: *Me too. That's actually why I joined the forum.*

Interesting. Maybe if we compare stories, we'll find some commonalities. Finally, I may be getting somewhere.

Me: *When did …. Um …. Delete. Delete. Delete. When were you a freshman here?*

Alex: *Two years ago.*

Sweet coffee stains. Have these rapes been going on for two years? Me: *And you were in the School of Social Work?*

Alex: *Yeah, I want to be a social worker.*

Me: *Me too! I graduated in the spring and am now working on my master's in social work.*

Alex: *Cool. Have you found a job yet?*

Me: *I work at the Youth Center here in town. Fingers crossed they'll give me a full-time position when I finish my master's.* No need to tell her my job there is guaranteed.

Alex: *I'm not sure if I'm ready to go back to school.*

Me: *What about taking one class – just to see how it goes.*

Alex: *I don't want to get near campus again.*

Me: *Hmm… what about online courses?*

Alex: *Maybe… in the future.*

Me: *It'll happen. You just need to have faith in yourself. And if you need anything, I'm always here.*

Alex: *Thanks. Gotta sign off.*

We quickly say our goodbyes. I sigh and lean back against my chair. This is going to be harder than I thought. I can't just question these victims. This is a place for them to come get support and feel safe – not to be grilled by yours truly. But that doesn't mean I can't find information about the rapes on my own. I go back to the *Introduce Yourself* thread and start reading.

Self-Serve Murder

An hour later I've read all the women's stories and my heart is breaking while my belief in mankind has plunged to new depths. It doesn't seem possible, but there are ten women in addition to myself who were roofied and molested in the past four years. All on campus. And no one has done a thing about it. The campus police are pretty much worthless.

A notification pops up and I read a message from the administrator asking me to introduce myself as well. I feel like an imposter as I type my story. I was the lucky one, the one who wasn't molested. Will it sound like gloating if I mention my virtue was left intact? Better leave that out. And I'm definitely leaving out any reference to waking up with a dead guy.

Chapter 6

Too much Monday. Not enough coffee.

I walk into the bakery on Monday morning and stop dead in my tracks. *That smell.* I want to somehow bundle that deliciousness up and sniff it whenever I'm feeling blue. I may be what Anna affectionately calls a coffee freak, but what woman doesn't love baked goods? Especially those slathered in chocolate.

"Hey, squirt," Anna yells her greeting from across the room where she's elbow deep in dough. Although with her height, it doesn't take much to be up to her elbows, whether it's dough or trouble.

"Is that Kristie?" Callie shouts before she rushes out of her nerd cave, also known as her office, which is usually covered in books on German literature. "Come on." She motions for us to join her.

I stall, trying to come up with an excuse to avoid what I'm sure will turn into an inquisition. These ladies do not let go once they latch onto a mission, and I'm afraid their new mission is to find out who drugged me. Before I can figure out how to get away unscathed, Anna arrives and starts pushing me towards the office. For a tiny thing, she sure is strong. Her obstinacy is like an additional power-pack as well.

She pushes me into a chair before plopping down on the other chair in front of Callie's desk, which is indeed overflowing with German nerd material. "So," she says as she rubs her hands in glee. "Did you find anything out?"

I want to lie. I feel totally uncomfortable discussing this stuff with my boss and co-worker, and besides, I don't want them to be targeted. Not only are they my friends who I don't want to see injured, but Ben and Logan wouldn't hesitate to eliminate me and bury the body somewhere no one would find it if anything happened to their women. But it's not like I can lie for a darn. And then there's the tiny matter of working in close quarters with these two nearly every day. No way I can get away with not filling them in.

I sigh. "Actually, I think I did find something."

Callie leans forward from her chair, putting her elbows on the desk and cradling her head in her hands. "What?"

"I found a forum for women who've been roofied and violated."

Boss-woman leans back in her chair and closes her eyes. "Oh my god. There have been enough students raped at the university that there's actually a forum for it."

Anna shakes her head sadly. "I don't want to believe it."

"Believe it." No one is more surprised than me to hear the steel in my voice. I decided months ago I was going to get to the bottom of these rapes. And yeah, maybe I despaired for a while that I wouldn't find out anything, but now I've got a starting point and I plan on using it.

Callie nods her head in approval of me. "What did you find out?"

"There were at least ten rapes," I state. "All the women were roofied and woke up back in their dorm rooms having been violated."

"Do we know if the crimes occurred in the dorm room?"

I shake my head. "I hadn't even thought of that." I hesitate before opening my bag and grabbing a bunch of papers. I took notes on everything I learned on the forum. I excluded any information that could possibly lead to a victim being identified, but still I struggle to hand the information over to Callie. I know she would never judge anyone and she'd certainly cut out her tongue before she gave information away. That doesn't change the fact that these women have already been violated and my giving away their information feels like another violation.

"You have more information?" Somehow Callie is now squatting in front of me. How long have I been staring at these pages? "It's okay, you know. You don't have to give it to me."

I nod. "I know, but I feel like you can help. It just feels like such a violation."

"Okay. You hold onto it then." She nods before moving back to her chair. "We should probably get back to work."

I stand and hand her the papers. "Promise me you won't try to find out who these women are." I keep my hand fisted in the papers until she nods.

"Callie!" Feet pound before Ben appears at the doorway. He smiles at her and she melts. Who can blame her? Ben in jeans and a t-shirt is hot, but Ben in a custom-made suit? Totally and absolutely drool worthy. He walks to her and leans over to give her a kiss on her forehead before turning to look at us. "Morning."

Logan walks in and immediately moves to Anna. "My pixie girl," he whispers before picking her up and kissing her neck. He sets her back in her chair and stands behind it with his hands on her shoulders. I'm tempted to roll my eyes at all the lovey-doveyness, but I've gotten used to it by now. If Logan or Ben are around, they are constantly touching or kissing their women. It's super sweet, especially since you don't expect it from the big, burly cops.

"So, listen," Ben says and interrupts my musings. "We have some information on the guy who was ... er... found in your bed."

"Yeah?"

"Turns out he was a fellow student at the

university. His name was Dick Reynolds. Name sound familiar?"

I shake my head. Ben nods in sympathy, but Logan is watching me with his hawk-eyes again. His look makes me feel guilty, even though I have nothing to feel guilty about. But that doesn't stop my mouth from opening up and defending myself. "I don't have much of a social life with working here and at the Youth Center. And of course college classes as well. I need to maintain a 3.5 GPA to keep my scholarship."

Logan nods and I feel like I just passed some kind of test. "Reynolds was majoring in social work as well," he adds as if I can get bonus points for passing yet another test.

"Undergrad?" Logan nods and I shake my head. "I wouldn't know him then, anyway. Not that I know many of my fellow grad students, but I don't have any classes with undergrads at all."

"What about the Youth Center?" Callie asks. "Aren't there other students doing their placements there?"

"I wouldn't ..." I start and quickly stop myself before I admit something I'm not planning to admit to these guys – ever. I shake my head. "I know all the students there, of course, but this guy. What was his name again?"

"Reynolds," supplies Ben.

"Reynolds wasn't one of the students doing a field placement there. Of that I'm sure. There's only one boy doing an internship at the moment."

"Okay, moving on." Callie taps her fingers on her desk. "What else do we know? How did he die?"

Ben sighs before answering. He knows better than to try to keep information from her. If he doesn't tell her, Callie would just figure out some other way to get the data. "It looks like he had some type of respiratory arrest."

"From the roofies?" I ask.

"You can die from roofies?" Anna's eyes widen in surprise.

35

I nod. "Especially if they are mixed with alcohol." I shrug. "And we were at a bar on Friday night." Wait a cotton-picking minute. I don't know that this Reynolds dude was at the bar. "Was Reynolds at the bar on Friday?"

Both Logan and Ben nod but Logan's the one answering. "Yeah. Witnesses place him there before midnight. He was pretty smashed."

I shake my head. "But that could be the effect of the roofie. Wait! Do we even know if he was drugged?"

"No. We're waiting on the tox screen for any drug or alcohol use."

Callie leans back against her chair and taps her chin with her fingers. "So we don't actually know it's murder at this point?"

Ben smiles and looks down at his girlfriend with obvious pride. "No. We're investigating it as a suspicious death right now."

"We? You're not homicide." Yeah, that sounded totally judgmental, but no one can fault me for wanting the men far away from the situation.

Logan snorts. "Like that will keep us away."

Burn the coffee! There's apparently no way I'm going to be able to keep the men and therefore my girlfriends away from this investigation.

Chapter 7

Some girls just want to have fun. I just want to have coffee.

After the boyfriends leave, Callie, Anna, and I get back to work. I go to the front of the bakery to open and start making that god-like liquid that is coffee while Callie and Anna finish the baking for the morning rush. Mornings are always super busy and the hours fly by until it's 10 a.m. and the place finally quiets down. There are some students chilling in the comfy chairs while doing some studying, but otherwise, the café is empty.

I'm wiping down the counters when I get ambushed by Callie and Anna. Callie grabs my arm and together with Anna she pushes me into the corner furthest from the students. "What in the world of coffee beans are you guys up to now?" I cross my arms over my chest to make it perfectly clear that I'm not okay with whatever cockamamie scheme they've cooked up now.

Anna looks at me and smiles in an obvious but unsuccessful attempt to look innocent. "It's just that we think it's time we see the Youth Center where you spend all your time."

Yeah, right. I roll my eyes at her. "You don't really expect me to believe that you want to see the Youth Center to check out my life's work."

Callie bobs her head. "We've been meaning to go down there for ages."

"Yeah," Anna jumps in. "Logan always makes it sound like the first circle of hell."

I raise an eyebrow at the troublemaking pixie. Of

course, she would want to jump into the first circle of hell. "Most people try to avoid Dante's Inferno." I don't know why I bother trying to dissuade her. She obviously has no fear of things 'normal' people avoid like gangs and violence and such. She even admits to starting to fall for Logan before she realized he was an undercover cop.

"We just need to make sure we can eliminate anyone from the Youth Center as possible suspects. You know – up close and personally – then we need to find this rapist before he strikes again. The dead guy in your bed was some kind of warning. It's time to get to the bottom of this." Callie makes an impassioned speech. I look down but, to my surprise, no soap box has magically appeared under her feet.

Unfortunately, Callie is right – as usual. The rapist needs to be found. And this whole thing just got personal. I might have backed off before Friday night since I wasn't making any progress anyway and my whole knowledge of the rapes was based on rumors. But now that I've been roofied and found out about the ten other girls who weren't as lucky as me? No way I'm bowing out of this investigation now.

"I thought you guys promised not to go to the Youth Center." I make one last ditch effort to keep Callie and Anna safely away from this investigation.

"I promised to not go running around. I will definitely not be doing any running." Anna shakes her head and points at her feet. As if those high-heeled boots would ever stop her from running head-on into turmoil.

Callie shrugs. "I never actually said the words 'I promise'. There's definitely some kind of loophole there."

"Fine!" I throw my hands in the air in defeat. "We'll head over in my car after the bakery closes this afternoon."

The dynamic duo immediately jumps up and down before rushing back into the kitchen giggling. And I'm the young one?

As soon as Callie locks up the bakery, we climb into my car and drive towards the Youth Center. The excitement I feel buzzing around the car starts to dim as we make our way to the area in which I spend the majority of my time.

"Flying fudgsicles," Anna mutters as her eyes grow bigger and bigger. "I didn't realize there were areas of the city that are this poor."

Of course, Callie, our resident walking encyclopedia, can't let that go. "About fifteen percent of the population in the city live below the poverty line. But the poverty line is controversial and somewhat arbitrary. Many experts argue that poverty is understated and that there are more households living in actual poverty than households which are below the poverty threshold."

Callie's lecture is fortunately interrupted by a jacked-up car with the stereo blasting away at levels that cause normal people's eardrums to explode flying past us. "Pink swirls of buttercream goodness," Anna exclaims. "This is like being in a movie." Her earlier trepidation is replaced by fascination as her rounded eyes try to take in everything at once as we move along.

"It's not a movie, it's real life." Uh oh, Callie's gearing up for another lecture. Luckily, we've arrived at our destination.

"Here we are," I announce as I hit the button on my remote control to open the gate for the parking area.

"This is the Youth Center?" Anna's head is plastered to the window as she takes in the building. It is a pretty awesome building. It's set away from the street and surrounded by a high fence, which is left open during the day and evening but locked up tight at night. The facility itself is brand new. While the parking is on the left side of the building, the right side of the building has a basketball court. There's also a climbing wall and obstacle course out back.

I park in my allotted spot near the side entrance and we climb out of the car. I see Callie taking everything in and hope she doesn't realize why I have such an awesome parking spot. I motion to them to follow me and walk to the entrance. I quickly swipe my card and open the door.

"After you, ladies," I say with a sweep of my arm.

"First circle of hell, my frosted bottom," Anna mutters as she passes me.

"Do you guys want a tour?"

"I'd love a tour. This is absolutely fascinating," Callie responds since Anna is still looking around with wide eyes and lolling tongue. If she had a tail, it'd be wagging in excitement.

"Just let me put my purse away." I quickly walk to the office and unlock the door with my key. One of the other interns is sitting behind a desk. "Hey, Eddie." I wave as I rush to my desk to put my purse away hoping he'll get the hint that I don't have time for him.

"Kristie, how are you?" No such luck. He stands and walks over to my desk where he leans against it before crossing his feet at the ankles looking for all the world as if he is settling in for a chat.

"Good," I say, keeping my eyes on my desk. I quickly unlock my drawer and throw my purse in. "I'm giving some friends a tour."

"Cool." I start to walk past him, but his words stop me. "Are you okay?"

I shake my head and force myself to stop walking. "What do you mean?"

"I saw you at Dylan's on Friday night. You were pretty smashed."

My heart starts to beat out of control. Does he know what happened to me? Does everybody? I don't need to be the talk of the university.

I force myself to look at him and smile. "I'm fine. Just a bit too much stress, not enough food, and way too much beer."

Eddie smiles in understanding. "It happens to all of

us. You can't be too careful, though."

I startle at his words. What does he know? "I'll see you later. My friends are waiting." I wave like a dork and rush out of the room.

"Okay," I say as I shut the door behind me. "Let's go."

"Who were you talking to?" Anna asks as she peeks around my shoulder. "He looks cute."

I ignore her and walk towards the locker room and showers. "Unfortunately, some of the kids have nowhere to get clean. We provide that for them."

"Hey boss-lady," is yelled as we move through the hallway.

I smile and wave before moving into the kitchen area. "Almost all of the kids who come here are underfed. We provide one meal a day. I... I mean *we* would like to provide three square meals a day, but it's just not in the budget at this time."

I point to a woman scribbling away at a counter in the back of the kitchen prep area. "That's the cook, Norma. Hey, Norma!" I wave hello and start to head out.

"Kristie, I had a question for you," she shouts as I try to make my escape.

"I'm giving my friends a tour and then I'll be back." I quickly scurry out of the room into the dining hall. The dining hall is nothing special. It has the same long tables and uncomfortable orange chairs seen in high school cafeterias across the country. But the lounge? The lounge is awesome. I walk through the double doors and have to stop myself from yelling *ta da!* Yeah, I love the lounge.

"This is the area where anyone can come and chill. Everyone is welcome. The only rules are no weapons and no gang colors." I point to the metal detector and security guard at the main entrance. The man is armed and could compete with Ben and Logan in the big and scary category. "There are always two guards present. One at the door and one roaming the facility."

The security guard sees me and waves. "Hey, boss-lady." I wave and push Callie and Anna in the opposite direction.

"Through here," I say with a sweep of my arm, "are the training rooms and counseling areas."

"Training rooms?"

"Yeah," I nod to Callie and keep walking. "We do all kinds of training here from anger management to ethics to computer skills." I point to a wall of windows where we can see into one of the training rooms. Class is in session and based on the writing on the chalkboard, they're working on remedial math. "We also do any and all necessary classes for kids who drop out to get their GED."

"Is there an age limit for the classes?" Anna asks with her nose pressed up against the glass.

"We help everyone up to and including twenty-year-olds," I say and nearly cringe at the pride in my voice. I'm not doing a very good job at keeping my secrets hidden.

Both Callie's and Anna's phones start ringing as I hear a ruckus at the front door. I rush to the front expecting to see some troubled kids trying to push their way in. It wouldn't be the first time. Unfortunately, Ben and Logan are facing off with the security guard who is pointing to the gun-free-zone sign in the window. *Sour coffee beans.*

Chapter 8

I only need coffee on days ending with a y

I quickly make my way to the front. "Roger," I say to the security guard as I place a comforting hand on his forearm. "It's okay. Ben and Logan are police officers." I nod to the two giants while smiling at Roger.

"But ma'am. The policy clearly states no weapons."

I nearly cringe at the whiney tone of the guard's voice. The man needs to be tough in the face of adversity and not act like a teenage boy. "Can you please show him your badges?" I plead with Ben and Logan. They nod and bring out their badges. Instead of quickly whipping them right back in their pockets – a horrible habit that should be totally banned – they allow my guard to review the badges. Finally, he nods and waves them through the entrance.

"Sorry about that guys," I say and start to look for an escape. I do not want to be anywhere in the same stratosphere as Callie and Anna when their men – who I'm pretty sure explicitly forbade them from coming here no matter what the trouble twosome says – find them.

Before I can make my escape, Logan grabs my arm and guides me towards the hallway where the girls are staring at their phones. They look up when they hear the heavy footsteps approaching. If I wasn't being guided by mister-scares-the-pants-off-of-me, I would laugh at the way they jump when they see their men.

Ben rushes ahead and grabs Callie's hand and pulls her to the door of an empty classroom. "We can use this room?" I quickly check the availability chart posted next to the door before nodding. We file into the room and Logan finally releases my arm but shoves me into a chair.

The ladies start to protest, but Logan quiets them with a look that scares the pants off of me but only makes them roll their eyes at him. Then, Mr. Scary himself turns to me and demands: "Are you going to tell them or do you want us to do it?"

I don't pretend I don't know what he's talking about. I'm not even surprised they know my secret. I cross my arms over my chest and scowl at him. "I'm pretty sure that's blackmail."

"I'm totally sure I don't care."

I resist the temptation to stick my tongue out at him and turn to Callie and Anna who are now sitting opposite me. Callie raises an eyebrow at me, but Anna just stares in obvious confusion. I sigh before blurting out my secret. "The Youth Center is in fact my Youth Center."

"Aha! I knew it!" Callie shouts before pumping her arm in victory.

"What?" Anna looks around at the faces in the room in confusion. "What's going on?"

I collapse against the back of the chair I'm sitting on and stare at the ceiling before revealing the last of my secrets to the two women I'm probably closest to in the world. "Well," I stutter. "It's not exactly true that my dad cut me off completely. I got access to my trust fund when I turned twenty-one, but instead of spending the money on college, I built this." I open my arms wide to indicate the center.

"What in the name of chocolate are you talking about?"

Callie smirks and turns to Anna. "She owns the Youth Center." She turns to me. "If I'm not wrong, she had the place built." I nod. "Which is why she was convinced the dead guy, Dick Reynolds, could not have worked here. She would to have hired him." If I wasn't so terrified with her reaction to the lies I've told them, I'd be impressed with

Callie's super intelligence yet again.

"But, but, but...." Anna mutters.

"What we want to know...," Logan interrupts from his position behind Anna where he's standing with his arms crossed over his chest and looking menacing without even trying, "... is why this is a secret?"

"And why didn't you mention this on Saturday? This is definitely a reason to target you," Ben adds.

I hold my hands up, palms out. The universal stop sign to indicate everyone should stop speaking now because I've had it. "Me owning the Youth Center has absolutely nothing to do with what happened to me and the rapes." I hear sounds of protest, but I ignore them and hold up my hand to start counting off the reasons they're totally and completely wrong. "First of all, look at how far we are from the university. Almost everyone who comes in here doesn't have wheels. Secondly," I continue with a sharp look at Logan. "You know gangs. Gangs don't drug women and then take them back to their dorm rooms. Even if I could get over a gang member drugging a woman instead of just taking what he wanted with violence, I cannot believe one of these guys would take the woman back to her dorm and tuck her into bed. And last but definitely not least, none of the women who were raped looked like they had been in a physical altercation except for ... you know." I blush as I trail off.

Ben looks at Logan who shrugs and then he turns his attention on me. "On Saturday, you said you didn't know that much about the rapes. You seem to know an awful lot more now. Care to fill us in?" He forms the words as a question, but it's perfectly obvious he's demanding to be filled in.

"I found a forum on the intranet. It's for women who have been roofied and raped."

Callie butts in before I can continue, although I'm not really sure what more I have to add. "But you didn't tell us the women weren't physically harmed except the actual rape."

I cringe. "Actually, I don't know if that's true. I only chatted with one of the women and she definitely didn't have any bruises or defense wounds."

"Okay," she nods. "That's something we'll need to check out in the future." Ben shakes his head at her but doesn't contradict her words, although I'm sure she'll hear about it later.

"Let's get back to Kristie's attack." Logan stares at me. "Is there anyone who holds a grudge against you since you own this place?"

I shake my head. "It's a pretty well-kept secret. I set up a company to purchase the land and build the building as well as run the center."

"What about the land purchase? Any fights over that?"

"No. There was already a Youth Center on this land, but the city cut the funds for managing the building and its employees and put the building up for sale. I snatched it up for a really good price."

"Anyone else interested in the location who could have been angry to be outbid?" Ben asks as he picks up Callie and sits in her chair before placing her in his lap.

I snort. "Seriously? In this area?"

Logan nods. "Yeah, property values in this area aren't exactly anything to write home about." He nails me with a glare. "Or to spend your inheritance on."

I roll my eyes at him. "Save it. I've already had that argument with my family about a million times. I don't need to hear it from mister-scares-the-pants-off-of-me as well."

Ben chuckles, but Logan just moves on with his interrogation. "What about disgruntled employees or students who didn't get placements?"

I smile. "My ownership is an extremely well-kept secret." I hear Callie snort, but I just plow on with my explanations. "All the employees have to sign confidentiality agreements as do the students. I interview the students as a fellow student and not employer.

Self-Serve Murder

Students only find out I'm the owner if they're selected for placement. They then sign confidentiality agreements."

"What about the school?" Callie asks. "Don't they know? You know how universities are like a hotbed of gossip."

I nod in agreement. "That's why they don't know. I'm employed here with the same forms and such as the other students."

"And other students who have been placed here? Any fights or disagreements?"

Anna laughs at that. "You have met Kristie, right? Nicest person in the world. Doesn't fight with anyone."

I smile at her before answering Ben's question. "In the first place, almost all of the students who work here are women. But I haven't had any arguments with any of the men either. In fact, several of our permanent workers are former students."

"So basically we're nowhere," Callie says and sticks out her bottom lip in an obvious pout.

Ben nuzzles her neck before responding. "Nope. We're eliminating possibilities. Sometimes an investigation isn't so much about following the clues as it is about eliminating suspects until one sticks."

Logan grunts in agreement. Well, if that's the case, I just hope the whole 'eliminating of possibilities' doesn't take forever because if Callie's right and the death of Dick Reynolds was meant to frighten me off then I just jumped smack dab into the frying pan.

Chapter 9

I'd stop drinking coffee, but I'm not a quitter.

I stand completely still with my fist poised to knock on my academic advisor's door, but I just can't seem to make myself move. I'm beyond embarrassed that he saw me in the hospital when I was at my most vulnerable. I'm pretty sure I wasn't imagining him leering at my breasts either. And what if he knows I woke up with a naked dead guy in my bed? I have no idea how long I stand frozen like a dork.

"Kristie! Hey, Kristie! How are you doing?" I turn and see Eddie, my employee who so helpfully noted my intoxicated state when I was at the bar, approaching me.

I shake my head at him and try to put a look on my face, which communicates my unfortunate inability to talk now because I'm, oh so busy. I also pretend not to notice the look of disappointment on his face and turn back to the door. I just barely stop myself from pounding on the door and manage to knock in what I hope is a dignified manner.

"Come in," is shouted from behind the closed door. I take a deep breath and enter Mr. Timmer's office. He looks up from his computer and gives me a huge smile. I nod in response, too freaked out to even bother trying to fake a smile. I've been dreading this appointment ever since he showed up at the emergency room. Is there anything more embarrassing than having a teacher, or semi-teacher in this case, see you nearly naked with only a thin hospital sheet covering you? I think not.

"Have a seat, Kristie," Mr. Timmer says and points to the chair across from his desk. I sit as he shuts his laptop and grabs a file from the huge pile on his desk. "How are you doing?"

I blush remembering the state of undress I was in the last time I saw him. Can this get any more awkward? "I'm okay," I mutter and quickly change the topic. "Have you had a chance to look at the list of courses I want to take next semester?"

I should have known it wouldn't be that easy. Timmer shakes his head and ignores my question. He leans forward. "Are you really okay?" He sighs when I remain quiet. "I may not know what happened but that doesn't mean I don't worry about you."

I am so not talking about this with my academic advisor! I squirm in my seat and try to come up with a way to get this meeting back on point. Timmer's phone rings and he sighs before reaching over and looking at the display. "I need to take this."

"Okay." I stand too quickly and my chair totters. "I'll just come back later." Total lie. Maybe I am a coward after all, but I'm getting the heck out of here. I don't wait for Timmer's response before backing out of the office. Thankfully it's a small room and I only have to take three steps before I'm back in the hallway. I hadn't shut the door on my way in, but I'm totally shutting the thing now.

⁂

After my cowardly lion performance at Timmer's office, I don't feel up to going to the Youth Center. I'm normally there every night checking on things, although I'm careful to keep the worksheets I turn into the university similar to the other interns doing their field placements at the center. Unfortunately, that also means that I only pay myself a salary for twenty hours a week. Luckily, I have my job at Callie's place.

I avoid everything and everyone and just head home. I'm restless and out of sorts. Too much nervous energy to actually get any studying done. I pull out my laptop and log onto the forum. I'm pleasantly pleased when I immediately get a private message from Alex asking me to join her in a private chat. I immediately open a chat.

Me: *Hey Alex! How's it going today?*

Alex: *I'm okay. Worried about you, though. How are you handling things?*

Me: *I'm doing okay but my boss and her friend have decided they're going to single-handedly figure out who .... hurt me.* I feel guilty typing the words 'hurt me'. Compared to what happened to Alex, my situation is a complete cake walk.

Alex: *Your boss at the Youth Center? You'd think they'd know not to get involved in a police investigation.*

I ignore the comment about getting involved in a police investigation, because isn't that exactly what she wants to do?

Me: *Not my boss at the Center. I have another job at a bakery.*

Alex: *Really?? Grad school, a field placement & a job?!?! Where do you find the time?*

I snort. Good question.

Me: *I don't have a social life.*

Alex: *Good.*

Spilled coffee! That's rude.

Me: *What do you mean – good?*

Alex: *Sorry, I just mean that you're amazing & so inspiring with everything you do.*

Me: **Blushes* Thanks*

Alex: *Anyway, back to your boss & friend. Isn't going after the bad guy dangerous?*

I shrug before realizing she can't see me.

Me: *Nah, their boyfriends are cops and this isn't their first rodeo.*

Alex: *Confused over here.*

Me: *Oh, sorry. My boss was accused of a murder she totally didn't commit. Together with my other colleague, they went off and figured out who did it.*

Alex: *Seriously? Is Veronica Mars your boss?*

Me: *Ha! Ha! More like Lucy and Ethel. But somehow they have solved two crimes.*

Alex: *I have to meet them.*

Me: *You should come to the bakery. I'll introduce you.*

Alex doesn't immediately respond and I worry I've pushed her too far. Based on our previous chat, I'm worried she's nearly a shut-in at this point. I'm starting to panic when Alex finally responds.

Alex: *Sure. Someday.*

I wipe my forehead in exaggerated relief and ignore her trepidation.

Me: *My boss and her bestie are totally cool but they are also crazy. I call them the troublesome twosome.*

Alex: *You call your boss troublesome?!?!*

Me: **rolls eyes* She's cool. Actually, she's a total nerd but for a total nerd, she's cool.*

Alex: *Nerd?*

Me: *Oh, yeah. She's a professor at the university as well. German literature. Need I say more?*

Alex: *Got it *winks**

Me: *So how are you really doing?*

Alex: *Taking it one day at a time. Gotta go. Chat later.*

She's signed off before I manage to type a response. I'm genuinely starting to worry about her. She seems perfectly normal except when I try to find out how she's really doing. Then, she completely shuts down. That can't be a good sign.

I'm pulled out of my reverie when there's a knock on my door. I shake my head when I look through the peephole and see the troublesome twosome in the flesh. I open the door and sweep my arm to indicate they should come in. "Ladies," I say with a snicker.

"Grab your stuff," Callie says as Anna grabs my purse and shoves it at me.

"What's going on?"

"The guys are meeting with campus police right now," Anna answers as she pushes me out the door.

"What?" I barely manage to get out of my apartment without falling. Talk about pushy.

"Ben and Logan are meeting with the investigators of the campus police about the murder."

I'm still confused. "What does that have to do with abducting me?"

Callie rolls her eyes at me. "Don't you need to fill out some kind of report with the campus police about Friday night?"

Still confused over here. "What? No. I already reported the crime."

Anna puts her hand on my chest to stop my retreat to my apartment. "Think about it. The boys are finding out information on the rapes with the campus police."

"Oh, my gosh." I can't believe these ladies. "You want to snoop."

"Duh." Anna releases me and we continue with our rush to the police station.

"How do you know your boyfriends are there anyway?"

Anna shakes her head at me. "Don't ask. Trust me, you don't want to know how Callie gets her information." By the blush Callie is now sporting, I think Anna's right. I do not want to know.

Chapter 10

Coffee helps me person. Personing is hard without coffee.

"So, what's the plan here?" I whisper to Callie as we enter the campus police station.

She shrugs. "You just go do your report. Leave the rest to me." Uh oh. That sounds like trouble to me. I look to Anna for support, but she's smiling and rubbing her hands in anticipation. Make that double uh oh.

"Can I help you?" I startle at the barked words. I slowly inch backwards, but Anna and her incredibly pushy hands are on my back urging me forward. Someone needs to remind me why is it that I hang around with these two.

"Um," I clear my throat, straighten my spine, and walk forward. "I need to make a report." I shake my head. "Well, I think I do. I'm not really sure."

"Oh, darling." The older woman sitting behind the counter switches off her bark and turns into a sweet, grandmotherly type. "Come with me. I'll take care of you." She stands and motions for me to follow her. I turn around for one last look at Anna and Callie, but I don't see them. Oh man, I don't want to be them when their men figure out what they're up to now.

I follow the woman to a small room with a table and two chairs. "Wait here, darling." With that, I'm left alone. I don't have time to have a full-blown panic attack before the door is swung open. A man who – judging by his plain clothes – is a detective swaggers in. I start to stand but he motions for me to remain sitting.

"I'm Detective Smythe," he announces as he turns

the chair on the opposite side of the table around and straddles it. I have to scrunch my nose to stop my eyebrow from lifting at his unprofessional behavior. "What can I do for you?"

I clear my voice and jump right in before I lose what little courage I have. *Think of the victims, Kristie. Think of the victims.* "I already made a report to the city police about what happened to me on Friday night, but..." I shrug my shoulders. "I'm not sure if I need to make a report here as well since it technically happened on campus."

"Ah," he nods. "You're the girl who woke up with the dead guy."

No amount of nose scrunching can stop my eyebrow-lift this time. Did he seriously just say that? Fortunately, he keeps talking because I'm sure whatever words were about to come out of my mouth would only lead to trouble.

"Look," he says as he leans forward. "There's nothing we can do about these cases. There's no evidence for us to work with."

I stand and put my hands on the table before leaning forward and glaring at Smythe. "So, you just do nothing. Women are being raped all over campus and you are the police. You're supposed to protect them."

Smythe has the gall to shrug before crossing his arms over his chest. "If girls are going to be stupid enough to go to frat parties, there's not much we can do about it."

I take a deep breath before I start to scream. He is wrong in so many ways that I don't even know where to begin. So I don't. Instead, I channel my father. I lean forward and in a calm but lethal voice tell him, "I'm going to have your job." I don't bother to wait for him to respond. I just walk out.

I hear shouting outside and head in that direction, but when I pass the woman at the desk, she stops me with a grip on my wrist. "My dear, if you need someone to talk with about..." She doesn't finish her thought but instead shoves a card into my hand. I scan the card and realize it's an invite for the intranet forum I found. At least that's one mystery solved.

"Thank you," I say and squeeze her hand. I'm about to ask her what she knows about the forum when the shouting outside increases. I shake my head as I realize that Anna is the one making the ruckus. I give the lady a smile before I walk outside to see what the troublemakers are up to now.

I nearly walk away when I take in the scene. Ben and Logan are standing next to each other with their arms crossed over their impressive chests. Their matching expressions are thunderous. They are not happy campers. They look scary as all get out. But that doesn't stop Anna. She's yelling at Logan and poking him in his chest. I hope she doesn't break her finger because I'm pretty sure his chest is made of stone.

"If you think for one minute you can stop me from trying to help these women, you're out of your cupcake-loving mind," Anna shouts while punctuating her words with poke after poke into Logan's chest. Logan actually rolls his eyes to the sky as if he's asking for patience.

Obviously, his request is denied as he grabs Anna's hand and pulls her flush with him. "And if you think that I'm going to allow you to be in danger for even one second, you're out of your freaking mind," he announces before crashing his lips down on hers. *Holy coffee!* That's hot. Maybe he's not so scary after all.

He comes up for air and declares, "I'm spanking that perky behind of yours if you get involved in this investigation." I change my mind. He's way scary.

Callie and Ben are having some kind of stare off. I wait, knowing Callie can't handle keeping her mouth quiet for long. "On average, only six percent of sexual assaults are reported to the police, Ben. Six percent. We know at least ten women have been assaulted." Her voice hiccups before she continues. "Do you know how likely it is that the actual number is way, way higher? You can't expect me to let this go. You know you can't."

"What I can't do is allow you to be vulnerable so that you become a statistic. I saw a mad woman try to run you down with her car." He shudders before continuing. "You can't expect me to allow you to get close to a serial rapist. I can't." Callie throws herself at him and he squashes her in his arms.

I clear my throat and walk closer to the group. Only a bit closer because the men are still radiating all kinds of *keep away* vibes. "What's going on?"

Anna turns away from Logan and huffs. "These guys dragged us out of the station. That's what's happening."

Logan leans down and whispers in her ear. "You're skipping over the part where we found you eavesdropping on police business." Anna shrugs and rolls her eyes as if eavesdropping in a police station is no big deal. To her, it probably isn't.

Callie walks toward me and grabs my hands. "How did it go?"

I shake my head. "Detective Smythe," I can't help but sneer his name. "Thinks the women were asking to get raped."

"What is it with the police in this town?" Anna shouts and throws her hands in the air. "Asking for it? I'll show him what asking for it looks like." She stomps toward the building but only makes it two steps before Logan catches her and throws her over his shoulder like a sack of potatoes. She immediately starts pounding on his back. He probably doesn't even feel it.

"Let me down!"

"Nope. You're done." He lifts his chin to Ben and takes off ignoring her screams and shouts. I see him whisper something into Anna's ear and put his hand on her back and she stills. I so do not want to know what he said.

"You okay?" Callie asks after we watch Logan throw Anna into his car.

I nod. "Oh, I did figure out one thing. The woman at the desk gave me a card with the information about the forum. So that must be how the other students found out about it."

"We should totally squeeze her for information." I laugh at Callie's use of terminology, but my laugh is cut short when Ben growls and prowls toward us.

"No more snooping," he says as he grabs her hand and starts to pull her away. At least he doesn't throw her over his shoulder. She waves as he drags her towards the parking lot. As soon as she's settled in the car, I turn and walk back to my apartment. Alex is not going to believe this.

Chapter 11

Coffee: Because crack is bad for you.

The second my computer is booted up, I get
onto the forum and see if Alex is around. I
know she said she had to go but that was hours ago.
Besides, I'm pretty sure she's on her computer more than
she's not. Sure enough, the little icon thingamabob
indicates that she's online. I immediately open a private
chat box and ask her to join me.

I don't bother with pleasantries.

Me: *You won't believe what happened?!?!*

Alex: *Are you okay?*

Me: *I'm fine but the troublesome twosome was at it
again*

Alex: *What did Lucy and Ethel do now?*

I snicker. I'm totally calling Anna and Callie those
names from now on.

Me: *They tried to snoop at the police station but
their boyfriends caught them!*

Alex: *Snoop at the police station? Are they crazy?
Why don't they let their men take care of things? They're
cops, aren't they?*

Me: **rolls eyes* Sure they're cops but that doesn't
mean we girls can't help*

Alex: *We? Are you getting into trouble now too?*

Me: *Don't you start too*

Alex: *You should leave the detecting to the
detectives*

Me: *I thought you wanted to find out who hurt you?*

When Alex doesn't immediately respond, I panic. For the love of coffee, I've gone too far.

Me: *Sorry. I shouldn't have said that.*

Alex: *It's ok. I just don't want you to get hurt.*

Me: *I'm safe. Don't worry about me.*

Alex: *Do you have a boyfriend to take care of you?*

Me: *Take care of me? I don't need a boyfriend to take care of me. I can take care of myself.*

Alex: *Sure you can but sometimes a man can protect you better.*

Sweet mocha latte! How do I respond to that? I totally disagree with that kind of sexism. But I don't want to isolate Alex any more than she already is. She never talks about herself. Does she have anyone to talk to besides the women in this chat room? I can't push her away. I'm just going to have to ignore her comment.

Me: *What about you? Any hot men in your life?*

Alex: *Nope. Gotta go.*

Oh, shootawhoota! That was stupid of me. I ended up pushing her away anyway. Every single time I try to get personal information out of her, she shuts down. I slap my forehead. Stupid. Stupid. Stupid.

———

"Okay, ladies," Callie calls from her office. "It's time for a sitrep. Get your butts in here."

A sit-what? I shake my head and head into her office, not bothering to ask her to clarify. I probably don't want to know the answer. Anna's already bouncing around in one of the chairs. I sigh and sink into the chair next to her.

"What's up?" I ask as if I don't know what Lucy and Ethel here are up to.

Callie ignores my question. "Did you learn anything at the police station?"

I raise an eyebrow at her. Me, did I learn anything? I was just reporting a crime and not snooping around before being thrown out by my police officer boyfriend. Of course, I don't say any of that and just shake my head. "I thought we already talked about this."

Anna snorts. "Like we could talk with the men around."

Um, okay then. "What did you guys find out?"

Anna makes a face. "Nothing. Stupid Logan has some kind of sixth sense or something and caught us before we could hear anything."

"Or he heard you giggling like a schoolgirl…" Callie shakes her head at Anna who responds by sticking her tongue out at her.

I quickly change the topic before things get out of hand with those two. "What were Ben and Logan doing there anyway? I didn't think they investigate murders."

Callie shrugs. "Who knows?"

Anna huffs. "Those two do whatever they want." I'm pretty sure that statement has nothing to do with Logan investigating the murder and everything to do with him carrying Anna off like she was a sack of potatoes yesterday.

"So we don't have any new information about the rapes at all?" I try to hide my disappointment, but I'm sure I totally suck at it considering the looks of sympathy coming from my boss and her bestie.

"Well, I know a few things," Callie answers and blushes. Anna snickers. Oh, man, someone's been up to her old tricks to get information. "There is no ongoing investigation into the rapes."

"WHAT?" I jump from my chair and start pacing. "You have got to be kidding me. We know of at least ten women who were raped and there isn't an investigation!"

Anna jumps up and hugs me. I try to shake her off, but apparently, she's been taking hugging lessons from an anaconda because I can't get rid of her. I feel another hand on me and look behind me to see Callie rubbing my back. "There are open case files, but no one's actually doing anything because there's no evidence."

I manage to shake the girls off and collapse in the chair. "That simply can't be true. I'm not some CSI person or anything, but there has to be evidence. You cannot tell me someone has committed ten rapes and didn't leave behind one bit of evidence!"

"Don't worry, girly," Anna says and grabs my hand before squeezing it. "We're on the case. Pixie and Nerd investigations to the rescue!" She throws one fist into the air and sings the last part. Oh, boy.

Callie shakes her head at Anna, but she has a huge smile on her face. She claps her hands together and puts on her professor-face. "We need to figure out the next step."

"I have no idea what to do. It's not like we have any evidence or clues or anything either." I'm whining, but who cares at this point?

My boss, the nerd, opens up a notebook and taps her pen on it. "Let's think about this. There must be some clue we're missing. Didn't the cop you talked to yesterday give anything away at all?"

I shake my head and try not to get angry when I think about that jerk who calls himself an officer of the law. "He just said that they didn't have any evidence and the girls were asking for it." Wait a cotton-picking minute! He did say something. I jump up in excitement. "I think the girls were all at frat parties before they were raped."

Callie tilts her head at me in question. "Why do you say that?"

"It's something the jerk-a-lot said. He said: 'If girls are going to be stupid enough to go to frat parties, there's not much we can do about it.'"

Anna jumps up and claps. "To a frat party, we go!"

I sigh and shake my head. "Actually, I already tried this. I couldn't find anything out."

Callie's eyes get wide. "You went to frat parties to try and find a rapist?" I don't nod. She's looking a bit too much like a mama bear right now.

Anna slaps my arm. "How could you?" I turn to her and she slaps me again. "How could you go all Nancy Drew and not tell us!" She's actually pouting now. I just stare at her.

"Ladies! Ladies!" Callie claps her hands. "Sit down." Unable to ignore that tone of voice, I practically fly into my chair. "This is what we're going to do." She points at me. "You're going to find us a frat party to go to this weekend." She turns her finger on Anna. "You're going to figure out outfits for us so we blend in and look like college students."

I can't help but point out, "I am a college student."

Callie snorts at me. "Let me clarify, a college girl who would be at a frat party." I roll my eyes at her. She stands. "Come on, back to the grind. We've got work to do."

It doesn't take much effort to find a frat party happening this Saturday. The frat boys sure like to advertise when they're having a happening. I told Callie about the party and we made plans to attend, but I absolutely, positively refused to let Anna dress me. The duo was shocked when I stuck to my guns. I have no idea why. My family thinks I'm the most stubborn person to walk the earth. Probably because I refuse to do their bidding. Nope. Not going to be a doctor. And, oh yeah, I'm using my inheritance to build a youth center in the absolutely worst area of town. Just call me Ms. Stubborn.

I'm just putting on the last of my make-up or rather re-doing my make-up before the dynamic duo picks me up. When you usually don't wear make-up, doing the whole smoky eye thing and not ending up looking like a raccoon is a challenge. Let's not even get into how often I poked myself in the eye with my mascara wand.

Self-Serve Murder

My phone beeps and I ignore it, assuming it's Anna telling me that they're almost here. It beeps again and I roll my eyes before setting down my eyeliner and grabbing it. It's a message from Alex. After our last chat, we both decided it would be easier to text each other rather than go through the forum. I've been using the opportunity to send her daily motivational messages as well as silly jokes to keep her spirits up. I swipe the screen and read the message from Alex.

Alex: *What you up to?*

Me: *Just getting all dolled up to go out*

Alex: *Do you have a date?*

Me: *Nah, just going with Lucy & Ethel to a party*

Alex: *What kind of party?*

Me: *Just a frat thing*

Alex: *A FRAT THING! Are you out of your mind?*

Me: *Relax. I'm going with Anna and Callie. We'll look out for each other.*

Alex: *But you know what happens at those frat parties!* I have no idea how to respond to that. Alex just keeps going. *Why are you going to a frat party anyway? You're not that kind of girl.*

I'm totally ignoring that condescending remark.

Me: *Chill out. We're just going to do a bit of snooping. Don't you want to find the rapist?*

Alex: *Gotta go.*

Oh, for the love of soy lattes! I know I shouldn't have asked her about finding her rapist, but she was really starting to annoy me. Sure, she's worried about me. That's sweet and all, but nothing's going to stop me from pursuing the rapist. Especially now that we suspect the rapist is a murderer as well. I shake my head and put my phone in my back pocket. Time to party.

Chapter 12

A real prince brings coffee.

I'm nervous as we walk the few blocks between my apartment and the frat house where the party is being held. Anna, on the other hand, is buzzing with excitement. I can't help but ask: "What did Logan say about you going to a frat party?"

She rolls her eyes at me and skips ahead. "You're crazy if you think I actually told him I was going to a frat party."

I shake my head. I can somewhat sympathize with Logan's need to haul Anna off over his shoulder from time to time. The girl is reckless with a capital R. "How are we going to do this?" I look at Callie for an answer.

"First of all, we're going to stick together. Secondly, we are not drinking anything at all. Promise me you won't drink anything." I nod and Callie smiles. She pulls a flask out and I have to wonder where she had that thing hidden. Her skintight dress doesn't exactly leave anything to the imagination, let alone room to hide a flask. "If anyone asks, we've got our own special brew." She hands the flask to me and I take a cautious sip.

"It's water?"

"Of course, it's water. We're on a mission. No alcohol allowed. That's rule number three."

Geez. How many rules are there? I'm just turning to complain to Anna when my name is called.

"Hey, Kristie!" Oh, lovely, it's Eddie. He's standing in front of the frat house and waving frantically to get my attention. It would be rude to ignore him. Man, oh man, I wish my parents hadn't raised me to be so darn polite sometimes.

I'm just raising my hand to wave when another man comes barreling towards me. "You're Kristie?"

He stops right in front of me and I look him up and down. "Do I know you?" I can't deny he's hot as in h-a-w-t, but I have no idea who he is. That doesn't stop me from perusing the man candy. He's tall, at least five inches taller than my five-feet-seven. And he's fit. His long-sleeved t-shirt is pulled tight across his chest and the sleeves are stretched to their limit over his biceps. He stands with his feet shoulder width apart and it's obvious there's some strength in those limbs.

"Alex," he says and I stop my perusal to look up at his face. His eyes are dark blue and sparkling with anger. What's that about?

"Alex? I'm sorry. I don't know you." I start to walk around him, but he reaches out and grabs my hand.

"Hey! Keep your hands off of her," Anna shouts and starts pummeling his back.

He chuckles. "This must be Lucy and Ethel."

"Lucy and Ethel?" There's only other one person who calls Annie and Callie those names. I gasp. "You can't be Alex. Alex is a girl!"

He releases my hand and steps back as Anna and Callie take up positions next to me. He puts his hands up, palms out as if to show he's harmless. Yeah, right. "Alex is my sister."

I shake my head. "Your sister tells you about her chats with me?" I find that hard to believe.

He blushes and looks at the ground; his feet shuffling in obvious discomfort. "No. My sister has never been on that forum."

"Look, mister, you better explain what in the world of coffee you're talking about before I sic Anna here on you."

His chuckle makes me want to scream. Only my desire to not draw any attention to our group, since we're only one house over from the frat party, holds me back. We're not exactly undercover, but a bit of discretion is advised when entering a party full of frat boys you plan to accuse of being rapists.

Alex, or whoever the man is, looks at Callie. "Is there somewhere quiet we can go to discuss this?" Callie, the traitor, nods and turns around. She grabs my hand and pulls me across the street before starting to walk to the coffee shop down the road.

No one talks as we walk the short distance to the café, which just leaves me plenty of time to try and figure out what in the world of coffee beans is going on. When I think of Alex, or whoever the macchiato the man is, going on the forum and pretending to be someone else, I want to scream. How dare he? Those women are fragile! They are looking for support, not some male predator. And why does he have to be so good looking? That's just rude.

Callie ushers us into the coffee house and immediately moves to a corner booth. I sit across from Mr. Mystery Man and just stare at him, waiting for him to fill us in on what he's up to. Because he's totally up to something. I don't know how long we sit there staring at each other before Anna breaks. "Are you going to tell us what is fudging going on or not?"

"Fudging?" He asks with a smirk on his face. I want to slap him. Hard.

"Stop delaying and explain who and what before Kristie has an aneurysm," Callie answers in a calm but hard voice.

He sighs and leans back in the booth. He runs a hand over his face before leaning forward again and stating, "First of all, my name is Tyler. Alex is my sister." I gasp. He looks at me with an apology in his eyes. "Everything I said about Alex and what happened to her is true." He collapses against the booth. "I just don't know what to do anymore. She moved back in with Mom and Dad and she basically won't leave her room. She has panic attacks if she goes outside so she just stopped going outside. She's twenty-one. Twenty-one!"

"That's horrible, Alex, I mean Tyler. But that doesn't excuse going on the forum and pretending to be her. The forum is a place for those women to get comfort and sympathy, not be trawled for clues."

He shakes his head and leans forward. He tries to grab my hands, but I quickly move them out of the way. "I promise I didn't bother any of those women for clues. I was actually planning on leaving the forum when you showed up. When you said you wanted to find who hurt you, I thought we could work together." I don't say anything, trying to work through the idea that Alex is really Tyler and Tyler is a boy. No, not a boy. A man.

"Besides," Tyler leans forward and whispers, "you haven't been exactly forthcoming either."

Beside me, Anna gasps. "How dare you?" she shouts before starting to squirm out of the booth. Callie stops her by pushing her back in the booth.

Tyler chuckles. "I think this one is Lucy."

I roll my eyes at him before getting back to the matter at hand. "What do you mean about me not being forthcoming?"

He blushes and looks at the table before answering. "I looked up the police reports for the night you were... you know... There was a murder that night." I don't say anything. Does he genuinely think I killed someone? What in the world? I thought we were friends. Okay, so I thought I was friends with Alex. Whatever.

"You can't possibly think Kristie had anything to do with the murder," Callie says in a voice which means business. She's probably plotting ways to murder him herself. Or, more likely, thinking of the most commonly used methods of murder.

Tyler holds up his hands in surrender. "No, no, that's not what I meant." He leans forward and whispers. "I know you woke up with the dead man."

I gasp and immediately try to flee. I start crawling

over Anna, but both she and Callie push me back into the booth. Callie turns on Tyler and hisses. "How could you possibly know that?"

He shrugs. "I'm a fireman. I have police connections."

Anna throws her hands in the air and starts muttering away. "What the cupcake? Not another one! How does this happen? We're strong, independent women. How do we keep ending up with these alpha men?"

I laugh and shake my head at her. "Talk about yourself. I don't have an alpha man."

Callie snorts. "Yeah, right."

I ignore her and turn back to Alex...er... Tyler. "So what are you doing here?" Because that's the real question, isn't it?

He crosses his arms over his chest and I can't help but notice the bulge of his biceps straining against his t-shirt until his angry voice hits me. "What do you think *you're* doing here? Going to a frat party to find clues! Do your men know where you are?"

Callie rolls her eyes at him and Anna bristles next to me. "What's it to you? We will do whatever we want!"

Tyler snorts. "Sure, until your man comes and carries you away."

Anna's spitting mad. Time to diffuse the situation before she jumps over the table. "Really? You're going to bring up things I told you when I thought you were your sister. Is that the way you want this to go?"

"Look." He runs a hand through his hair before continuing. "I'm sorry about that. I didn't mean to hurt you. But it's a good thing I did. Otherwise, you would be at the frat party unprotected right now."

I growl. Yes, growl. Talk about a back-handed apology! "I'm done." I push Anna and she moves out of the booth. I follow her out and start walking to the exit with Callie and Anna hot on my heels. "We'll have to reconvene and do this another time."

"Over my dead body," Tyler swears from behind us.

I ignore him and keep walking. Once we're outside on the sidewalk, I turn to Callie and Anna. "I'll see you guys tomorrow morning at work." They nod and send furtive glances toward Tyler. I ignore the glances and wave before turning and heading back to my apartment. What a waste of a night!

Chapter 13

I'm not addicted to coffee, we're just in a committed relationship.

I can hear Tyler following me the short distance to my place, but I ignore him. Only when I reach the entrance to my apartment building do I turn. "Look, I won't tell anyone what you did on the forum, but it's best if you delete my info from your contact list." Before I manage to turn and stomp away, he grabs my elbow and stops me.

"If you think I'm leaving now, you're out of your mind."

Who does he think he is? I shake his hand off my arm. "What is your problem?"

He steps closer and crowds me against the closed door. "My problem! What's my problem? How about the fact that you were obviously targeted by a serial rapist? How about the fact that the dead boy was obviously a message for you to back off? How about the fact that you haven't backed off and are running off half-cocked acting like some sort of private detective? And what about the fact that no one's protecting you?"

What is it with the men in this city? Why are they always trying to suffocate women? I roll my eyes at him and turn back towards the door without bothering to reply. I pull on the door to open it, but Tyler smashes his hand on the frame to keep it shut. I turn back to him. "I don't know who you think you are, but it's time for you to let me go into my apartment before I call the police." I would never call the police on him, but he doesn't need to know that.

He releases the door and crosses his arms over his chest. "Fine. I'll just stand guard out here."

I look around the dismal front yard of the apartment building. It hasn't snowed yet this year, but the grass is covered with a layer of frost which will only thicken as the night progresses. I look at Tyler and realize he's not even wearing a jacket. He must be freezing! "Why aren't you wearing a jacket? It's December in Wisconsin! Have you lost your mind?"

"I barely had time to get dressed when I found out you were on your way to a frat party!"

I raise an eyebrow. "So it's my fault you're freezing?" I shake my head and turn back to the apartment. "Come in and get warm and then you need to leave."

I open the door and walk to my apartment without looking back. After I get into my apartment, I walk to my tiny kitchen and fill the kettle with water. "Do you want cocoa or tea?" I ask as I continue to move around the kitchen.

"Coffee's good."

I look up to argue with him about drinking coffee before going to sleep and notice he's taken off his shoes and is stretched out on my sofa. "What are you doing?"

"Getting comfy," he responds and picks up the remote control to turn on the television.

I stomp over to the sofa and grab the remote from his hand. "I said you could get warm and then you need to leave."

"If you think I'm letting you sleep in this apartment alone again before the murderer is found, you're wrong."

"How dare you?" I throw the remote into the chair. "Fine. I'll call Ben. He can deal with your stubborn butt."

That gets his attention. He stands and stalks toward me. "Good. I want to talk to him about leaving you unprotected when it's obvious you're being targeted."

Oh, great. I can either call Ben and have him come

over here to get into a fight with Tyler or put up with Tyler being in my apartment. "Fine!" I say with a stomp of my foot. "Get your own coffee. I'm going to bed." I turn and take the three steps to go from my living room to my bedroom. I hear a chuckle behind me and for the first time in my life, I'm tempted to give someone the bird. I do give into the temptation to slam my door.

I hide in my bedroom the next morning until I absolutely have to leave in order to make it to work on time. Finally gathering all my courage, I open the door to the living room, but it's empty. Guess I was hiding for nothing. I rush to Callie's, hoping some hard work will get the infuriating man out of my mind. I should have known it wouldn't be that easy.

The morning rush is just finishing when Anna and Callie attack. "So, Kristie, what happened with the hottie last night?" Anna rushes right in.

"Did you talk about his sister and what he was doing on the forum? Did you learn anything new?" Of course, Callie's got her eye on the prize. She's not going to be distracted by some man candy. No wonder it took Ben over a year to even get her to go out on a date with him.

Anna smacks Callie's arm. "Stop being serious. I want to know where hottie slept last night."

I immediately blush and Anna gasps before grabbing my arm and pulling me into the kitchen. "Did something really happen?"

Not what she thinks. I shake my head. "No, he slept on the couch. He wouldn't leave."

"Why didn't you call us? I could have made him leave."

I can't help but laugh at Callie. She wouldn't have done anything besides tell her boyfriend to get a move on. And that's exactly why I couldn't call. Not that I'm sharing that information or anything. "It's fine. He's gone now."

Self-Serve Murder

Callie leans against the prep table and crosses her arms over her chest. "What are we going to do now? I hate to admit it, but Tyler may be right. Going to a frat party might not exactly be a safe move."

I shrug. I have no idea where to go from here.

"What about the drugs?" I turn at Anna's question.

"What do you mean by that?"

Callie interrupts before Anna has a chance to answer. "Do we even know what drug it was?"

Guess I forgot to tell them the hospital called with my blood results. "Yeah. Just like I thought. It was Rohypnol."

"Maybe we can find someone who has a prescription or something for Rohypnol."

I shake my head at Anna's suggestion. "I've already researched that before you guys even joined this three-ring circus."

Callie ushers us into her office. "What did you learn?" She asks as soon as she's pulled out her notebook.

"The drug Rohypnol isn't legal in the U.S. so there's no way anyone would have a prescription for it."

"But then how is *he* getting the drug?"

"That's easy. You order it online for five bucks a tablet," I answer with a sneer in my voice.

"That's horrible! Can't the FDA or the border police or immigration or someone do something about it?"

Callie ignores Anna's outburst. Instead, she's sitting at her desk tapping her pen against her notebook. I can practically see the wheels of her brain turning from here. "What is it?" I ask when she continues to stare off into space.

It takes a minute for her to respond. "We're assuming that whoever killed that Dick Reynolds guy is also the rapist, right?" Anna and I nod in agreement. "What if we're going about this the wrong way around? Instead of trying to find the rapist and therefore the killer, maybe we should find the killer who also happens to be the rapist."

I look at Anna in confusion but she just shrugs. "I have no idea what you're talking about."

"Let's look into the murder of Dick."

Anna claps and nods. "Yes! Let's find a killer!" Oh, man, she's gone off her rocker; assuming she was ever on it that is.

"I thought you agreed to keep your noses out of the murder." Ben and Logan can be way scary when their women disobey them. I don't want any part of that.

No one even bothers to respond to my statement. Instead, Callie starts throwing out orders. "Dick was a student in your college, right?" She keeps going without waiting for my confirmation. "Kristie, you're in charge of trying to find out more about him. Maybe get his file or something."

"Hold up!" I stand and put my hands on Callie's desk right in front of her. "Why don't you get his file? You're a professor and have access to private information I can't get to."

"Nope," she says with a shake of her head. "The files are all kept divided between colleges. I can only get information on students in the College of Letters & Science. Dick was in your college."

I hate it when she's right. "Okay. I'll see what I can find out. What are you going to do?"

Callie's face colors a bit before she answers. "I'll see what I can find out about how he died."

"And I'll see if I can find anything out about the ongoing investigation," Anna adds. I turn away from her before she sees my smile. There's no way Logan will tell her anything about an ongoing investigation.

"Okay then." Callie claps. "Everyone knows what they need to do. Let's get to it."

Chapter 14

I may not cry over spilled milk, but I'll lose my freaking mind over spilled coffee.

Luckily, the bakery is only open half-days on Sundays. I didn't get much sleep last night with Mr. Pushy sleeping on my couch. I could totally go for a nap. I practically sleep walk home from *Callie's Cakes*. I walk into the building and immediately stop when I see Tyler casually leaning against the wall across from my apartment door. There's a sport's bag at his feet. That can't be good.

"What are you doing here?" I try to remain calm.

"Until the murderer is caught, you're stuck with me." So much for calm.

"What in the name of caramel lattes are you talking about? You said one night. You've had that night." Is this my punishment for being relieved he was gone this morning?

He chuckles. Chuckles! I'm about ready to start screaming and he flipping chuckles. "I never said one night."

I stomp my foot and open my door. He grabs the bag to follow me. I turn and shut the door in his face. "Stay out there!" I yell through the door.

Callie picks up on the first ring. "Hey, Kristie."

I bang my head against the door. "I need your help."

"What's going on? Should I bring Ben?"

"Oh, yeah, you definitely need to bring Ben."

"On our way."

I throw my phone on the kitchen counter before divesting myself of my coat, hat, and gloves. I leave my boots on. My feet are ready to be freed from the confinement of my boots, but there's no way I'm confronting Tyler in stocking feet. Time to make a bunch of coffee because knowing Callie, Anna and Logan will be joining our merry group as well.

"Who are you and what you are doing in front of Kristie's apartment?" Yep, Callie definitely called Anna because that's Logan's scary as day old coffee voice.

I rush to the door and open it wide before I lose my security deposit due to blood stains on the carpet in the hallway. Logan and Ben are staring Tyler down, but he's not backing down one tiny bit. That bloodshed is looking more and more likely. I clear my throat, but the men don't bother glancing in my direction. They keep their eyes on Tyler and chin lift in my general direction, which I'm pretty sure translates to something like *we know you're there but we got this*. Yeah, right.

"Get in here! I'm not losing my deposit because you decide to go all MMA in my apartment building."

Callie grabs Ben's hand and drags him into the apartment. Anna tries to do the same, but Logan doesn't go anywhere he doesn't want to go. But then Anna steps between him and Tyler and Logan growls at her. She just cocks her head at him, completely unafraid of the caveman in front of her. Meanwhile, I'm shaking in my boots. Yep, keeping the boots on was the way to go.

Logan grabs Anna's hand and pulls her behind him before walking backwards into my apartment, keeping his eyes on Tyler the entire time. This is exactly why I let Tyler stay last night. I didn't need this macho posturing then and I don't need it now. When everyone is in the apartment, Tyler remains standing in the hallway.

"Not coming in?" Maybe it was easier to get rid of him than I thought.

He shakes his head. "You didn't invite me in."

I roll my eyes. "Get your behind in here now."

He chuckles and I have to fist my hands to keep from slamming the door shut in his face. The man is freaking irritating. "I liked you better when you were a girl." Ben and Logan burst out laughing, but Tyler growls. Oh, great, he can growl too.

I indicate the chair for Tyler to sit in. He immediately sits and then pats the arm of the chair indicating I should join him. No way. I shake my head. I'm not stupid enough to sit that close to him.

"What's going on here?" Logan demands. I raise an eyebrow at Anna, but she shakes her head. She hasn't told him a thing. That's a surprise.

"This is Tyler." I sweep my hand out to indicate the man who is currently relaxing in my chair as if nothing were amiss. "He posed as Alex, his sister, on a school forum that was set up for the rape victims."

Logan lifts Anna off his lap before standing and gently setting her down on the sofa. As soon as she's settled, his gentleness is history and he stalks to Tyler. "You did what?"

Tyler springs from the chair and stands toe to toe with Logan. Not one bit afraid of the scariest man I know. "I didn't have a choice. My sister is twenty-one-years-old and she gets panic attacks so bad, she's become a shut-in. I'm hoping that if I find her rapist, it will give her some kind of closure and she can move on with her life again."

Logan nods in what looks like understanding. Ben joins their little huddle. "Did you find anything out?"

Tyler shakes his head. "Not really. There were ten women on that forum." He looks at me. "Well, eleven now. All of who were ..." he looks away from me, "... raped." Oh, no, he thinks I was assaulted. "There doesn't seem to be any pattern to the attacks. Some women were at frat parties while others were at a bar." He looks at me when he says the last part.

I shake my head and walk to him. "Um, Tyler. I

think there may be some kind of misunderstanding." He just continues to stare at me with this look of utter devastation in his eyes. I feel my face flame, but I trudge onward. "I was drugged, but I wasn't … um… violated."

"You're sure?"

As if I wouldn't be sure that I'm still a virgin. "Yeah." My face flames, but I trudge on. "I've never even …" I shrug as my words taper off.

He blows out his breath and looks to the floor. His body seems to deflate right in front of me. I'm not sure what's going on. After a moment, Tyler moves. He turns to me and grabs me in a tight hug. His arms wrap around me and he squeezes until I can barely breathe. "Thank god," he mutters over and over again.

I put my arms around him and squeeze him back because he obviously needs this. We stand like that in my living room for who knows how long. Finally, I feel him take a deep breath and stand up straight. He gives me one more squeeze before releasing me. He looks down at me and smiles. I can't help but gasp at how utterly gorgeous he looks with that smile on his face. He has two dimples on each side of his smile. Of course, he has dimples. He reaches up and tucks a strand of hair behind my ear. "Thank god, baby."

I roll my eyes at the term of endearment and step away from him. Dude obviously hasn't had his coffee today if he's calling me baby. I clear my throat. "So anyway, Tyler here thinks he can stay with me until the murderer, rapist, whoever is caught."

I tap my foot and wait for Ben and Logan to defend me. Instead, they smile and turn to Tyler to give him chin lifts. *What the…?* Ben claps his hand over Tyler's shoulder. "Excellent idea. I've had patrol cars doing extra drive-bys, but I'd feel much better if someone was here with her."

Logan nods in agreement. "I've had my crew keeping an eye out for her as well, but I agree, it's better if someone stays with her." He moves back to the sofa and picks up Anna before sitting down and placing her on his lap as if he didn't just order a stranger to stay with me.

"But he's a stranger! And he pretended to be his sister!"

Ben and Logan look at each other, obviously doing some kind of silent alpha man conversation. Logan nods and Ben looks at Tyler. "Obviously, we'll run a background check." Tyler nods at Ben's raised eyebrow.

I look at Anna and Callie to back me up, but they just stare at Tyler and refuse to meet my eyes. "Fine!" I shout as I throw my arms up. "I'll stay at the Youth Center then."

Growls fill the air and it feels like the oxygen just got sucked out of the room. I ignore the feel of danger in the air and stomp towards my bedroom to throw some stuff in a bag. I don't get far before Tyler grabs my hand and pulls me to him. "You're not staying in the Youth Center. It's not safe."

I scoff at him. "I own the place. There's security twenty-four-seven and besides, the local boys won't hurt me."

"We'll talk about the fact that you didn't tell me you own the Youth Center later." I roll my eyes at that directive. He shakes my arm in response. "You know it's not safe, so stop posturing and deal with it. I'm staying here."

I look over my shoulder at my boss and her bestie. "Callie? Anna?"

Callie stands. "I agree that you shouldn't be alone." I start to protest, but she throws up a hand to stop me. "But if you feel uncomfortable with Tyler here, you can stay with us. I can put a cot in my office."

I nod. A cot will have to do because there's no way I'm staying at Anna's place. Logan may be protective of me, but he still scares the snot out of me.

Tyler shakes me again. "You're not staying on a cot. You work two jobs and finals are coming up. You need to be more comfortable than sleeping on a cot. If I make you feel so uncomfortable, I'll sleep in my truck."

Oh, great, now I'm the one feeling guilty. It gets flipping cold at night in December in Wisconsin. And that's before taking the wind chill into consideration. "Fine. You can stay on my couch." He smiles and his dimples come out to play. I narrow my eyes at him. "If you lie to me again, though, I will take great pleasure in demonstrating just how it is that women manage to get silky, smooth legs. Bald would look good on you. Probably."

Chapter 15

I'm just waiting to see if my coffee uses its power for good or evil today.

Although I slept in my normal 'respectable' pajamas of flannel shorts and t-shirt, I throw on an over-sized sweatshirt and a pair of jogging pants before heading into the living room. Tyler doesn't need to see my braless state or my bed hair for that matter. Bed hair! I turn back to my bathroom and quickly finger comb my hair before throwing it in a ponytail. I cautiously open my bedroom door, hoping that my houseguest is either asleep or missing. No such luck. He's standing at my kitchen counter staring at the coffee machine as if it's going to jump up and bite him at any moment. He turns around when he hears the door.

"Baby," he says with a smile. "You can wear as many layers as you want. You'll still be beautiful." I feel my face heat up and he chuckles. I've about had it with this chuckle of his. I especially don't like how it makes me want to smile at him.

"Staring at the coffee machine isn't going to work. You have to actually turn it on and push buttons and stuff." I move past him and grab the cup next to the sink to fill the water reservoir.

"I have no idea how to use that thing."

Now it's my turn to chuckle. "Is that your way of making sure you never have to make coffee while you're here?" I open the machine and fill the water up.

Tyler moves up behind me and crowds me. With

his hands on the counter on each side of me, I'm trapped by his big body. "That's my way of asking you to teach me how to use that monstrosity so that I can make coffee for you tomorrow morning and every morning after. So, I can take care of you."

Wow! Is it suddenly warm in this kitchen of mine? How dare he be super sweet! Can't he just stay a pushy jerk? I can deal with pushy jerk. Super sweet, I'm not so sure I know how to handle. "Don't you need to get to work or something?" Yes, those are the words that finally escape my mouth.

He chuckles. Of course, he chuckles because I'm being ridiculous. "Baby, the sun isn't even up yet. The only people who need to be at work at this time are farmers and fisherman."

"Then, what are you doing up?"

Another chuckle. "Baby, your alarm isn't exactly quiet."

Well, that's true. I may have a teensy tiny obsession with the snooze button. Oh, no, the snooze button. I hit it one time too many this morning. "Shootawhoota! I need to get to work." I leave the coffee beans and cups where they are and rush off to my bathroom for a shower.

I'm surprised, although I shouldn't be, when I rush out of my bedroom to find Tyler dressed and ready to go. "Where are you off to?" I'm rushing around grabbing my keys and bag while trying to shove my feet into boots and put on my coat and don't hear his answer. "What?" He didn't just say he's coming with me, did he?

"You heard me," he says and then treats me to the two-dimple smile. That smile should totally be registered as a lethal weapon.

I don't bother answering and hurry out of the apartment. I'm turning towards the bakery when Tyler grabs my arm. "You're not walking," he declares. I roll my eyes. What is it with him ordering me around?

"It's only a few blocks." It's like I didn't even speak.

Self-Serve Murder

Tyler pulls me to his truck and makes sure I get in before running around to the driver's side. It doesn't take five minutes to make it to *Callie's Cakes.*

When we arrive, I turn to him and note: "The bakery isn't open for another fifteen minutes."

"No worries. I'll wait out here until it's open."

I shake my head and jump out of the truck before heading to the back entrance of the bakery. Anna's rolling out dough on a table when I open the door. She turns to me and smiles. "Bow chica bow wow. How's Tyler? Where's Tyler?"

I want to ignore her because Anna is fifty shades of crazy, but I've learned in my life that you never ignore crazy. "In the car."

She immediately lifts her hands from the dough and rushes to the back door. She peeks out before turning back to me. "You seriously left him in the car?"

I shrug. "It's not like I asked him to go all bodyguard on me."

Anna giggles and goes back to her dough without saying another word. Looks like miracles really do happen. I walk through the bakery and enter the café to prepare for opening. I take down chairs, turn on the coffee machines to warm them up, and prepare the cash in the till. At 6 a.m. on the dot, there's a knock on the door. Tyler is standing there with his dimples on display, pointing to his watch. I shake my head but open the door.

I manage to ignore Tyler brooding in the corner during the morning rush. It's Monday, which means that we're busier than normal. Everyone needs an extra shot of espresso on Monday morning. As soon as it calms down, Tyler's up and moving to me. Oh, boy.

"I need to head to work, baby. I'll be back before you close up this afternoon."

I lean over the counter and whisper. "Can you stop with the baby stuff? I'm not your baby."

"Oh, baby, you totally are," he declares before

turning around and strutting right out of the place.

"I'd let him call me baby," Anna declares from her place in the doorway where she's fanning herself.

"Liar. If you let anyone besides Logan call you baby, he'd spank your behind."

She giggles and blushes. It's flipping adorable with her pink hair and tiny stature. I thought I was just kidding about the whole spanking thing. Maybe not.

"Anyway," I say with a shake of my head. "I'm out of here. I have class this morning."

She walks over to me and whispers loud enough for everyone in the entire building to hear, "Are you going on your secret mission as well?"

I sigh and nod. "At lunchtime." I have no idea, but I figure the administration office where student records are kept will be the least occupied at that time. I still have no coffee-colored clue how I'm going to get Dick's file.

When my morning class ends, I slowly gather my things instead of throwing everything in my bag and rushing out like the building's on fire, which is my normal routine. My classroom is only a few doors down from the administration office and I want to be super-duper sure that everyone from this class is good and gone before I start my snooping mission. I sincerely doubt I can find anything about Dick Reynolds out, but if Callie and Anna can solve mysteries then so can I, darn it.

In order to make sure enough time has passed, I spend some time in the bathroom refreshing my non-existent make-up and emptying my already empty bladder. I can't think of any more delay tactics. Guess it's time to earn my snoop-master wings.

I try to walk normally to the administration office, but I'm tiptoeing like an idiot. I just can't seem to help myself. The outer door of the office is open and I slip inside. There's a high counter separating the students from the staff, but no one is manning the counter at this time of day. I peak around, but I can't see anyone in the office. I slowly walk around the counter and look around. If I were a student file, where would I be?

"Hey, Kristie." I grab my chest and turn towards the voice. It's Eddie – again.

"What are you doing, Eddie? Are you stalking me or something?" My voice may be a little bit harsher than I intended, but the boy did just scare the daylights out of me.

"Um...," he mumbles as his face turns a bright red color. "No. I just wanted to see if you want to go out with me this Friday. We can hit a movie or maybe have dinner." He looks up at me with eyes that can only be described as a lost puppy-dog. Shoot.

"Well," I draw the word out as my mind searches for an excuse to turn him down. I nearly shout ah-ha when I come up with the perfect excuse. "I'm kind of seeing someone."

His eyebrows fly off his forehead. "You are? But you haven't dated anyone before."

I ignore the fact that he seems to know my dating history. "It's complicated, but I think he wouldn't be happy with me going out on a date with anyone else right now." That's not a total lie. Tyler would be annoyed with me dating some right now. Not because we're dating or anything, but because he's taken on the role of big brother protector until the murder is solved and the rapist found.

"Kristie?" A voice mutters from behind me. I spin and see Mr. Timmer exiting one of the offices. Holy moly! He was here the whole time. Good thing my snooping attempts were interrupted by Eddie's date proposal.

"Oh, hey, Mr. Timmer," I say with false brightness as I slowly walk to the other side of the counter. "I was just looking to see if anyone was around, but I forgot it was lunch time." I giggle. Yes, giggle. My life just gets more and more embarrassing.

"There's no one here right now."

I nod in response. "I'll come back later." I turn and

85

start marching out of the office.

"We still need to re-schedule your appointment," he shouts as I speed walk down the hallway.

"I need to get to work. Gonna be late. I'll call you." I don't bother looking around to see if Timmer hears my words and I totally ignore Eddie calling my name. I'm outta here.

Chapter 16

"Be strong," I whisper to my coffee.

Tyler slips into *Callie's Cakes* just as we're closing. I'm not sure if I'm annoyed or not. I spent the entire last hour waffling between wanting him to show up and hoping he wouldn't. My head's a mess. Just what I need with finals around the corner. Plus, there's that pesky little matter of finding a rapist who may indeed also be a murderer. And yippee! He may be targeting me.

"Hey, baby." He leans forward and kisses my forehead. Darn it, why does he have to be sweet? "How was your day?"

I don't call him out on calling me baby again and decide to poke the bear instead. "Interesting. Got asked out on a date." I don't add that I get asked out more often. I want to poke the bear, not incense it by waving a fresh steak in its face.

Tyler rushes me and I'm forced to walk backwards until I'm squished between the counter and the wall of muscles from the man in front of me. "What did you say?"

I'm not sure if he's asking me to repeat myself or for my reaction to being asked out on a date. I go for innocent. "I said I was asked out."

A sound scarily similar to a growl comes from his chest. "I heard you the first time. What did you tell the little jerk?"

I'm not going to put up with that kind of prejudice. "Hey! Don't call Eddie a jerk. He's a good guy. In the social worker program and works with me at the Youth Center."

"He works with you," Tyler practically growls the words.

"Duh. That's what I just said. I hired him because he seems to genuinely care about those kids." With each word I speak, he presses closer and closer to me. I try to wiggle away from him, but he has me totally immobilized.

"We still need to talk about you owning the Youth Center and not telling me." I roll my eyes at him. He seems to think I'm under some sort of obligation to tell him everything. Just a few days ago I didn't even know he was a boy. I start to call him out for his lies, but he shushes me with a finger over my lips. I have the weirdest compulsion to bite it, but I manage to control myself. "For now, let me just make it clear that you won't be going out with him."

I roll my eyes at him. "Yeah, yeah, I know you want me all wrapped up in bubble wrap or something until the rapist is found."

He shakes his head at me. "You really don't get what's going on here, do you?"

"Besides you being super annoying?"

He chuckles and those dimples come out to play again. I'm becoming obsessed with those dimples. He leans forward to kiss my forehead. "No, baby, you're mine."

Not the right thing to say. "I belong to no one."

Tyler ignores my response. "Already thought you were cute based on our chats with all your talk of Lucy and Ethel and lord knows you have a heart of gold but the first time I caught sight of you? I knew I was going to make you mine."

There's that word again: mine. Trying to possess someone is not sexy no matter what all those romance books say. I manage to duck under his imprisoning arms and quickly scramble to the kitchen.

"We'll talk about this when we're home." I can hear his shout through the door, but there's really no response to that sort of disillusionment.

Anna grabs me and pulls me into Callie's office. She shuts the door before pushing me into a chair.

"So." Callie stares at me from across her desk as she impatiently drums her fingers. "What did you find out?"

Oh, man, they are going to be way disappointed in me. I shake my head. "Nothing. I didn't even manage to find where the files are kept before Eddie walked in on me and then Mr. Timmer appeared from one of the offices."

"Who's Eddie?"

"He works at the Youth Center and is in the same program as me."

Mission forgotten, Anna leans forward and whispers. "Is he cute?"

Where is this coming from? Does she have sex on the brain or something? I shrug. "I guess. I never paid much attention. Although…" I shut up when I realize I was about to reveal that he asked me out.

"Although what?" She's nearly bouncing out of her chair now.

I sigh. Might as well tell them. I already told Tyler anyway. "He did ask me out today."

"Oh!" She claps her hands before falling back into her chair. "What did you say? What did Tyler say? Did you tell Tyler?"

I wave a hand at her in an attempt to get the questions to stop. "You know I don't date."

She rolls her eyes at me. "Is that like a steadfast rule? And why don't you date anyway? It's time for you to get over what those stupid high school boys did. High school boys are stupid. Scratch that. Most boys are stupid. They're trainable, though."

I laugh. Seriously? As if she could ever train her man. I ignore her uncomfortable questions about my dating history or should I say lack of dating history? I decide to throw her a bone. "I said no. I lied and said I was dating someone."

Callie and Anna snort. "You are dating someone," Callie pipes in with her two cents.

I shake my head. "Um, no, I'm not. I think I'd know

if I were dating someone."

Callie rolls her eyes at me. She looks at Anna. "Should we just let her figure it out by herself?" Anna nods and Callie turns back to me. "So no intel at all?"

Intel? What is she? A secret spy working undercover as a cupcake bakery owner? "No. What should we do now?"

"Social media," Anna answers and Callie nods as she opens her laptop. "Let's see what we can find out."

I'm not really sure how information learned about Dick from social media will help the situation, but they're the experts. Well, not authentic experts, but they somehow managed to bumble their way through two murder investigations. I sit and wait for what they come up with and try not to think of Tyler and his declaration that I'm his. Men. Completely clueless.

"Kristie, Kristie!" Anna snaps her fingers in front of me. Guess I spaced out.

"What?"

She shoves a list of names at me. "Do any of these names sound familiar?"

I don't bother looking. "Who are these people?"

She shakes the paper in front of my face. "Facebook friends of Dick who also go to school here."

I quickly scan the paper but no names jump out. "Wait! Eddie's on this list."

"Loverboy, Eddie?"

I roll my eyes at her. "How old are you again?"

Callie speaks before Anna gets a chance. "Can you talk to him? Find out if Dick was up to anything before he was murdered?"

"I guess." Not like it's going to be awkward or anything after I just turned down a date with him.

"Hey, Kristie!" Tyler yells before knocking on the door. "Don't you need to get to the Youth Center?"

"Oh, shoot!" I shout as I jump up. "I need to run.

We'll pick this up tomorrow." I shove the list in my back pocket before rushing out of the room. I nearly run straight into Tyler, who is standing in the kitchen leaning against a counter with his legs crossed at the ankles.

"Come on," he says as he straightens and grabs my elbow. "I'll give you a ride."

"Just can't shake you, can I?"

"Nope." He winks and those darn dimples come out to play.

Chapter 17

Of course, size matters. No one wants a small cup of coffee.

"Don't you need to go to work or something?" I finally blurt the question out in frustration as Tyler drives while humming a happy tune. What does he have to be happy about?

"Trying to get rid of me?" Uh, yeah.

"At this point, I think getting rid of an actual leech would be easier." He chuckles for a second before going back to the happy humming. "Aren't you going to answer my question?"

"Who added cream to your coffee?"

I can't help it. I burst out laughing. I expect the big guy to use colorful language that will make me blush, not the dorky stuff about coffee I say.

"This is the Youth Center?"

I ignore the question and pull the remote control for the gate out of my bag. I push the button and the gate opens. "Park there," I tell him; pointing to the spot next to the employee entrance. There's no sense in pretending I don't have the best parking spot in the lot since he already knows I own the place. As soon as he puts the truck in park, I jump out and head for the entrance.

"Where's the fire?" Tyler asks from right behind me.

"Really?" I raise an eyebrow as I turn to him. "A fireman making fire jokes." He shrugs but doesn't answer as he follows me into the building. I walk to the office and spy Eddie sitting behind a desk through the door. I quickly initiate Operation-Get-Rid-of-Tyler-Now. "Thanks for the lift. See you later."

Tyler shakes his head at me but doesn't bother to respond to my comment. How the heck am I going to get rid of him? I'm on a mission from the cupcake girls to get some information from Eddie, but that's not going to happen with Mr. Overprotective in the building. Time to spin a little tale.

"Can you wait somewhere else, then?" He raises an eyebrow at me but doesn't say anything. I huff. "I need to discuss things with my employees, private things." It's actually true. Not only are the counseling sessions here private, but we also have a rule that we keep all information about who comes and goes from the building confidential. "There's a lounge with an obnoxiously large television through there." I point down the hallway and to the right. "You can talk to whoever you want, but any information you learn in this building stays in this building."

Tyler cups my chin and leans down to give me a kiss on the forehead. "Sorry, baby. Of course, I'll leave you alone to get your work done." I let the breath I was holding in escape as he marches off.

"Hey, Eddie," I greet as I finally enter the office.

"That's the guy you're dating?" Was he watching us through the door?

I shrug. "Kind of." Even if I don't want to date the guy, I don't want to lie to someone I consider my friend as well as employee.

I throw my bag on my desk and then walk over to Eddie. I lean against his desk and hope it looks nonchalant. "So, I need to ask you something."

Eddie smiles. He's cute when he smiles. Nowhere on the level of Tyler but not bad. And why am I comparing Eddie to Tyler? I shake my head and start again. "Did you know Dick Reynolds?"

"Yeah, I was in a lot of classes with him."

How do you interrogate someone about a friend? No clue. "Do you know what happened to him?"

93

He shrugs. "Rumor on campus is that he overdosed."

I'm still amazed that the fact that Dick was found dead in my bed has escaped the rumor mill. I know Ben and Logan worked on some scheme to keep all the information about what happened to me that Friday night and how I woke up on Saturday morning on the down low. I just find it hard to believe that they managed to trick the college rumor mill. Something I was sure was impossible. "Did he use?"

"Nah." He shakes his head. "I mean, I don't know for sure, but he didn't seem the type, you know?"

I nod in agreement. "I guess you just never know."

"Why are you asking about him?"

Hmmmm…. How to answer that without exposing the whole found-a-dead-guy-naked-in-my-bed thing? I shrug. "Just doesn't seem to add up to me. I interviewed him for a job here. He didn't seem like a drug user."

Eddie squints at me as if trying to judge if I'm being honest or not. I am being honest, just not entirely truthful. "Well, there is this one thing," he starts. I lean forward.

"Well, isn't this cozy?" I startle and nearly fall forward into Eddie's lap. With as much dignity as I can muster, I turn around and smile at the intruder.

"Mr. Timmer," I say with my professional smile firmly in place. "I didn't know you were here."

He raises an eyebrow and shakes his head in disappointment. "That's obvious." Geez, what does he think is happening here?

I ignore that comment. I know what it looked like, but just because he saw that doesn't mean it's Timmer's business. "How are you doing? Here to check up on Eddie? Or the Youth Center?" In addition to advising students, helping them select their specialization and giving them guidance about career opportunities, Mr. Timmer also does routine checks at the places where students do their field placements. It's a chance for the advisor to see if the organization is meeting the requirements for field placements as well as to check up on students.

"I thought I'd do some checking on the Youth Center, Ms. Larson." Using my last name? Oh, yeah, he's disappointed in me. What I don't know is why.

"Sure, Mr. Timmer. Whatever you need." I walk to my desk and take a seat. "What do you want to go over?" As soon as Timmer walks to my desk, Eddie jumps from his chair and bolts out the door. I must not be the only person having trouble with the advisor. It can't be easy to be an advisor. College kids can be nearly as volatile as the little wannabe gang members who walk the halls of the center.

"First of all, we need to re-schedule your last session. You need me to sign-off on your final classes and project." Timmer takes a seat across from my desk.

"Yeah, we do." I ignore the way my face is heating up from the memory of his visit to the hospital and grab my day planner from my bag. I flip it open. "What day works for you?"

Timmer responds, but I don't hear him. Instead, I hear the shouting coming from the day room. I jump up and run out of the room with Timmer hot on my heels. I walk into the room to see Tyler and Eddie squared off. They're both standing with their arms across their chest and faces full of anger. Uh oh. I quickly walk forward and stand between the two of them.

"What's going on here?" I ask the room in general.

Tyler doesn't respond, just continues to try and burn Eddie with his glare. "I have no idea," Eddie responds. "I just introduced myself to this guy and he went off on me."

Yeah, I can see that happening. I probably should have told Tyler that Eddie's working today instead of shuffling him off with promises of oversized televisions. "You both need to tone it down. I expect this behavior from teenagers, not two grown men."

I hear snickers and look over to see a group of teenagers sitting in the corner. They have huge smiles on their faces. I shake my heads at them. "Shows over," I tell them and they immediately pout before heading in the direction of the kitchen.

"You two gonna behave or do I need to send you to the naughty corner?"

Tyler chuckles, but Eddie isn't amused. "I didn't do anything."

I sigh and nod at him. "I know. Why don't you head into the kitchen and make sure those kids don't eat us out of house and home?" He nods but then stomps off, making sure everyone in the entire building is aware of his anger.

I ignore Tyler and turn to Mr. Timmer. "It's not usually like this," I start apologizing. He's not listening to me, just staring at Tyler as if he's a puzzle. "Oh," I shake my head to rid myself of the embarrassment. "This is Tyler. He's helping me out for a few days."

"Helping out with what?"

Tyler ignores his question and throws an arm over me. "Kristie's mine. I wanted to come and see everything she's accomplished with the Youth Center. It's amazing." He turns to wink at me. "As is the woman herself."

"Yes, yes, she is," responds Mr. Timmer.

I glare at Tyler. How dare he declare I'm his possession in front of my advisor? Who does he think he is? Before I can decide how to respond to the man, his phone rings. He kisses my forehead before walking off to answer it. I take a second to take a deep breath before turning back to Mr. Timmer. I plaster my professional woman face on. "Let's get started, shall we?" I say and walk back to my office, trying hard to not stomp. I may not have been all that successful.

Chapter 18

On the bright side, my coffee will never get cold in hell.

"I'm telling you there's something up with Eddie," Tyler says for like the millionth time since we left the Youth Center yesterday. And I thought I was stubborn! I continue to ignore him and open the door to the bakery for my morning shift.

"Morning, Anna!" I shout as I walk through the area with Tyler following me.

"I'm serious. Listen to me. It's gotta be him."

Now, I've had it. I turn to him and point my finger at him. "No, it doesn't 'gotta' be him. The only reason you think Eddie had anything to do with the rapes is because he asked me out. Asking me out isn't a crime." I poke him one final time in the chest and he grabs my hand.

"If I had my way, it would be." He actually growls the words.

I roll my eyes at him and pull my hand. He's not letting go, though. Of course, he's not. "Let me go so I can get to work."

"No! You're going to stop ignoring me and we're going to discuss this."

I throw my free hand in the air and look to the ceiling and ask if there's anyone up there willing to help. Getting no reply, I look back at the totally infuriating man in front of me. "There's nothing to discuss. He asked me out. I said no. End. Of. Discussion."

"Not that I'm not enjoying the show but what's going on?" Anna giggles as she stands there watching us but not wading in to help.

"Mr. Big Bad Fireman here thinks that Eddie is the rapist just because he asked me out."

"You have to admit it's suspicious."

Oh, no, he didn't. I glare at him. "Are you saying that I'm not worth asking out? That someone would only ask me out because he's a rapist?"

Tyler must realize his mistake because he releases my hand and starts to back up. He puts his hands out in front of him as if to signal his surrender. I don't think so. "Um, no. I'm saying that the guy seems to be showing up everywhere. That's suspicious."

"You idiot! He goes to school with me and he works at the Youth Center with me. Of course, he's at those places! It's not like I ever see him outside of those places." Except I did. Once. He was at the frat party. I totally forgot that until this very moment. I still, wondering if it's possible that Eddie is indeed the bad guy. Tyler crowds me the second he feels my hesitation.

"What is it? What are you thinking?"

"He was at the frat party," I whisper.

Tyler grins in triumph. He actually grins. Before he has a chance to open his mouth and insert his foot, Callie saves him. "I don't think he did it." I whip my head towards her. Where did she come from?

"Why not?" Tyler's back to growling.

"Sit down and I'll explain." She points to the chair in the office behind her and waits for Tyler to move before walking to her desk and sitting down.

The moment Tyler's behind hits the chair, he barks, "Explain."

I move to stand behind him and squeeze his shoulder. By the amount of tension he's radiating, I worry he's thinking of his sister. It must be tearing him upside that he hasn't found the man who hurt her yet.

"Kristie gave us all the information about the women on the forum." She blushes before continuing. "I looked up all the women."

"You did what?" If it were possible to chop her head off with laser beams pointing out of my eyes, she'd be headless right now.

She holds up her hands. "I didn't give anyone the information or anything. I was just trying to find some sort of pattern."

I gasp when I realize what she's saying. "You found one."

"Not exactly. There are some commonalities, though. We already knew all of the women were studying social work."

I nod. "Yeah, because the forum is only available to students or alumni of the social work school."

"And it turns out all of them were undergraduates when they were assaulted." I clear my throat. "Except you."

"That doesn't mean that Eddie didn't do it." Tyler is holding on to his belief that Eddie is guilty undeterred by the lack of evidence.

Callie turns to Tyler and nods. "Yeah, but the fact that the rapes have been occurring for four years and that Eddie is only a junior kind of does."

"Four years? How in the world is it possible that someone has been raping undergraduates for four years and no one has noticed anything?" Apparently, I've turned into a crazy person as I'm shouting my questions.

Callie sighs and gets that look in her eyes. The one that proceeds her foisting facts upon unsuspecting listeners. "Over eleven percent of college students experience rape or sexual assault. Only twenty percent of female students report their attack to law enforcement and even less seek assistance from victim services."

Tyler leans forward. "So we don't even know if all the women on the forum were assaulted by the same man?"

"I'm not finished." Callie gives him her lecturer stare until he nods. "The women were all roofied and returned to their dorm room. That's too much of a coincidence for there to be several attackers."

Everyone is silent for a few minutes while we digest this new information. "So what are we going to do now?"

"We're going to go through the rest of the list and talk to the rest of Dick's friends."

Anna snorts. I didn't even realize she'd joined us in the room. "You mean Kristie is going to talk to Dick's friends."

"What? Why me?"

"They're all students as are you. You can ask questions as a fellow student. Maybe make up some story about writing some kind of article to honor him in the college newspaper." Anna's just full of ideas when she doesn't have to do anything herself.

"You want me to lie and say I'm writing an article for *The Daily Cardinal*, but in reality, I'll be interrogating Dick's friends." I'll never admit it aloud, but it's actually not a bad idea. There's got to be a reason Dick ended up dead in my bed. I shut my eyes to erase that horrible image from my mind. "Okay, I'll get started tomorrow."

"Not without me you don't."

I roll my eyes at Tyler's declaration. "Who's going to talk to me about Dick with you standing near me acting all Mr. Macho Caveman?"

Mr. Caveman himself stands and stalks towards me. He crowds me until I'm forced to back up and run into the wall. "You are not interviewing male students without me there. End of discussion."

Anna and Callie giggle and I'm pretty sure I hear someone whisper 'told you so' under her breath.

"Whatever." It's not like the man can follow me around twenty-four-seven. He needs to go to work at some point. At the very least, he needs to take care of bodily functions sometimes.

Chapter 19

You can do it ~ whispered my coffee

I've spent the entire night plotting and planning and I've come up with the perfect plan to get rid of Tyler so I can question some of Dick's friends. Its genius is in its simplicity. Genius might be ever so slightly overstated. I normally leave the initial interviewing of candidates for field placements at the Youth Center to my manager. This time I'll be interviewing the candidates myself and what a select group it is.

Bang. Bang. Bang. "Kristie, don't you need to get to work soon?"

"Nope, I don't work this morning." I open my Youth Center file and pull up the standard email to invite candidates to interviews. The door opens and I squeak. "You can't just come into my bedroom," I shout before quickly shutting my laptop and turning to Tyler.

"I knew you were dressed," he says with a shrug. I raise an eyebrow at him. "The shower turned off ages ago."

"So? Maybe I was taking my time getting ready? What if I was just walking around naked?" Not that I'd ever do that or anything, but he doesn't need to know that.

Tyler chuckles and shakes his head. "Baby, as much as I would love to see that, we both know you don't walk around naked."

I blush but plow forward. "How in the world would you know that? You don't know me!"

He grins but doesn't bother responding. Instead,

he walks forward and places a cup of coffee on my desk. "Good morning, baby." He wraps a hand around my neck and squeezes before placing a kiss on my forehead.

He's nearly at the door before I gain my voice. "Seriously, Tyler, don't you need to get to work?"

"Nah, baby, I'm all yours. I took some vacation days."

"What?" I quickly walk over to him and grab his arm. "You can't take vacation days for this."

He smiles at me and those danged dimples come out to play. "Baby, I have to make sure you're safe. Can't fight fires if my mind's distracted."

Of course, I know Tyler is a firefighter, but I never gave any thought to how dangerous a job it is. I swallow the lump that suddenly appears in my throat. "I don't like that you have a dangerous job." I don't even realize I said the words out loud until Tyler moves and encircles me in his arms.

"I'm careful, baby. I promise you. I'm careful." He leans back and looks down at me. "Gotta say, I love that you're concerned." His lips lightly brush mine. There and gone again before I even realize what's happening. He smiles before releasing me. He turns me around and pushes me back to my desk. "Get back to your work, baby. I'll make you some breakfast."

And now I feel guilty for the whole deceive Tyler thing. Goodness gracious, that man can turn me around. Sighing, I open my computer and get to work on the email invites. I hope no one finds it odd that the interviews are scheduled the day after the invitation is sent.

The next day I'm set up in the conference room the college makes available to recruiters. This whole thing better not blow up in my face. It's not like I expect to keep my ownership of the Youth Center secret forever. Once I graduate, I won't be hiding the fact anymore. But I still have one semester to go and I'm not willing to reveal my secret yet. Let's hope these friends of Dick's buy my little white lie that I'm just working there and have been tasked with performing the initial interviews to see if they fit in with the current team.

The first 'candidate' arrives and the guilt immediately seeps into my bones. He's dressed up in a suit and tie and looks nervous as all get out. Can you say Wicked Witch of the West? That's me alright. I swallow my guilt, force a smile on my face, and stand to greet him.

"Hi, I'm Kristie, I work at the Youth Center." It's not a lie. I do work there.

His hands are clammy and my guilt ratchets up again. "I'm Kevin."

For the following fifteen minutes, I go through the standard interview questions. Yes, standard interview questions. Callie read some study about unconscious bias in hiring practices and now I feel obligated to use the same questions for every candidate regardless of their responses. When I said it wasn't necessary, my boss asked me if I wanted to be part of the problem or part of the solution. We know who won that argument.

"Okay," I say as I close my notebook. "Thanks for coming in, Kevin." I cough before jumping into the real reason I've asked him here. "By the way, did you know Dick Reynolds?"

"Yeah, I was in a bunch of classes with him."

I didn't really think past that initial question. I guess I should have prepared for the 'interrogation' as much as the interview. Oh, wait, didn't Anna say something about writing an article? "Did you know him well?" Kevin just shrugs. Very helpful – not. "It's just that I'm thinking about writing an article for *The Daily Cardinal.* Some sort of tribute or something." He nods but doesn't jump in with any spontaneous information. Darn it. "Can you tell me anything about him?" I lean forward and whisper. "I don't believe he was a drug addict or whatever everyone is saying."

That finally gets a reaction out of the man. He

103

laughs. "Nah, Dick was a total lightweight. A couple of beers and the guy was off his rocker. Drugs would have made him sky-rocket."

I sigh in relief. "Any funny stories or anything you can tell me about him? I want readers to know what he was really like."

"Dick was a goofball. He was always playing practical jokes. I think he actually kept a whoopee cushion in his backpack. Man, Professor James was beyond mad when she sat on that thing." He chuckles and shakes his head.

"Is there anyone he pulled a practical joke on who wanted to get revenge?" Is it possible Dick was killed for a reason other than the rapes? Have we been looking at this wrong the whole time?

"Nah, he embarrassed people, but it was all in good fun. He wasn't nasty with his jokes or anything. He never picked on anyone in particular. I'm pretty sure everyone in Introduction to Social Policy sat on the stupid whoopee cushion at least once." Kevin stands, obviously finished talking about Dick.

"Well, thanks for coming in." I walk him to the door and watch him walk down the corridor. Three more interviews to go.

Two hours later, I'm starving and about to scream in frustration. I've learned nothing about Dick except he wasn't the best student and was quite the wisecracker. It sounds like Dick was the last man on earth I would have wanted to talk to, let alone invite into my home and bed. On the upside, the interviews weren't a waste of time. I've now learned that there's no way in the name of Columbian coffee I would ever hire any of these guys. None of them are ready to be out in the real world. They're still all a bunch of kids joking around in classes. I'm surprised they're even in the social worker program. None of them seem the type. Callie would say that's my unconscious bias speaking. Someone needs to get that girl a hobby that doesn't involve learning boring trivia.

"So, did you learn anything?" I startle at the sound of Tyler's voice. Sneaky man.

"What do you mean?"

He shakes his head and leans against the door. "Is that how you want to play it?" I shrug. There's no possible way he knows I interviewed Dick's friends as a pretense to find out information about Dick. How could he? "Just because I'm a fireman doesn't make me stupid."

"What?" His jaw is tightened in anger. "Are you mad? I never said you were stupid! And frankly, I can't believe you don't know me better than to think I judge people based on their jobs."

"Sorry. So now will you tell me if you learned anything?"

I scrunch my eyes and stare at him. "Why do you think I was trying to 'learn' anything?"

"Baby, every single person you interviewed was a man. You're the one that told me that male social workers are rare."

I sigh. "Fine. They're Dick's friends."

"And?"

"And nothing. I didn't learn anything about Dick except the guy was apparently a practical joker and didn't take his studies seriously. I have no idea why anyone would murder him, assuming he was murdered." I grab my stuff and try to walk past Tyler. He's having none of that. He grabs my arms and pulls me into a hug.

"We'll find out what's going on, I promise," he whispers into my hair before pressing a gentle kiss on my forehead. And then he leans down and seals his lips to mine.

Chapter 20

I'm tall, dark, and fantastic in the morning ~ says coffee.

I don't even bother trying to get rid of Tyler the next morning. I merely allow him to drive me to work without any grumbling. That may be because he fixed me coffee, made me breakfast, and then kissed the daylights out of me. I can still feel my lips tingling. And I thought that whole lips tingling thing was a lie made up by romance novelists.

"Kristie," Anna whisper-shouts from the door separating the café from the bakery kitchen when the morning rush is over. "Do you have time for a sitrep?" I look over at Tyler who is talking on the phone with his back turned towards me before nodding and following her into Callie's office.

Callie leans forward with her elbows on her desk. "So," she wiggles her eyebrows in excitement. She shouldn't ever do that again. "Did you find anything out from Dick's friends?"

Of course, Lucy and Ethel know that I interviewed a few of Dick's friends yesterday. I can't keep anything secret from them. Even if I managed to hide something from the duo, Tyler would rat me out. I sigh. "Not really, except I don't think I would have liked Dick much if I had ever met him in person."

Callie drums her fingers on her desk. "So why was Dick the man who was murdered and put into your bed as a warning?"

And just like that, I've had it. I jump up and start

pacing the tiny office. "How do even we know Dick was murdered? Maybe he just took a sip of my glass by mistake? He was a practical joker. And – judging by his supposed friends – totally immature. Maybe he thought it would be funny to drug someone and see what would happen? We have seriously no idea what's going on. We don't even know if the rapes have anything to do with Dick's death."

Somewhere in the background, I hear Callie speaking. "Ben, you need to get down here now. Kristie is having a complete freak-out."

"And these rapes? According to Callie, the walking encyclopedia, rapes are happening all the time on college campuses. I can't even think about that." I shudder before continuing my rant. "But that means that the rapes are probably not connected at all. And who knows why in the world I woke up drugged with a freaking dead man in my room." I think I may have screamed that last part.

Tyler bursts into the office and immediately engulfs me in a hug. "What did you do to her?" I'm surprised he can get the words out of his mouth with his teeth clenched like that.

Anna shrugs in response. "Who knows? She lost it when Callie started asking her questions."

Tyler growls at Callie. "Hey!" Ben yells as he joins our merry group. "Don't you dare growl at my woman." He struts over to Callie and kisses her forehead before tucking her into his side for safety.

"Sorry, man," Tyler mumbles, but I feel how his body continues to vibrate with anger.

"What's going on in here?" Oh, great, Mr. Scary has decided to join the show. Anna squeals and jumps into his arms. He must be used to it because he leans back on one leg to balance his weight as she jumps.

"Apparently, your women are harassing mine," Tyler grunts with no regard to his safety at all.

I push against the wall of muscles encircling me, but Tyler's not letting me go. "Stop it! It's not their fault. I

107

was just having a little freak out is all."

He turns to me and gently brushes my hair from my face. "Why, baby? What's wrong? You seemed fine when we got here."

I shrug. "It's just that I've been thinking about everything and nothing makes sense. How do we know those rapes were related? We don't even know that Dick was murdered. He could have taken those drugs himself."

Ben clears his throat. "We can clear up that last part for you at least." I turn to see Ben sitting in Callie's chair with Callie perched on his lap. "The autopsy is done and the case has been declared a murder investigation."

"Why? I mean, if you can tell me."

Anna grunts. "Of course, they can tell us. You woke up in bed with murdered dude. That must give you some rights or something."

Logan shakes his head at the pixie, but he's smiling at her and suddenly I understand the attraction. Because, that smile? Wow. Just wow. "The autopsy confirmed he died of respiratory arrest caused by a lethal overdose of Rohypnol. His high blood alcohol content probably contributed to the effects of the drug."

I nod. That's pretty much what we assumed from the beginning. "But how does that prove it's murder?"

Ben takes over the explanation. "It doesn't, but it's suspicious enough that his death is now a murder investigation."

"Suspicious how? Couldn't he have just taken the drug himself and screwed up the dosage? Isn't it used to create a 'super high' or something?" From my research, I know that heroin and cocaine abusers use Rohypnol to produce profound intoxication – the 'super high'.

"True, but it's illegal in the US and there is no evidence whatsoever of Reynolds buying the drug or using the drug previously."

"Plus," Logan pipes in. "Those who use it to create intoxication usually don't drink heavy amounts in addition to taking the drug. And we know he didn't have heroin or cocaine in his body at the time of his death."

I'm still not buying it. "It sounds circumstantial at best."

Ben smiles at me and shakes his head. "Sometimes that's all you've got to go on."

"Okay, I'll agree – for now – that Dick was indeed murdered, but what about the rapes? We've been assuming they're all related and therefore committed by the same dude, but we don't really know that. Ms. Know-It-All over there says that eleven percent of college students are raped."

Callie grimaces. "This is where I have to admit I was wrong." I gasp. "Well, not wrong exactly, but not completely and properly informed."

"Get on with it." The woman could spend an hour explaining why exactly she wasn't wrong if we let her.

"Although it's true that approximately eleven percent of college students are raped, the number of those who are raped because they are incapacitated by drugs is significantly lower. It's beyond frustrating because apparently, there are hardly any studies being done on this issue." She shakes her head in disgust. "Anyway, in those studies which have been done, it turns out that Rohypnol is the least popular drug to use as a date rape drug."

"Wait. What? I thought roofies were the most prevalent date rape drug."

Callie shakes her head again. "No. That would be GHB."

That's shocking. Everyone talks about Rohypnol being *the* date rape drug. The term is roofied after all. "So you're saying that you think the rapes are definitely connected because of the use of Rohypnol."

Logan answers. "Not only that but the other factors as well: all female students in the social worker program, all victims were returned to their dorm rooms, and woke up alone and naked."

There's something important to what Logan is saying. Some clue I'm sure I'm missing. But my phone rings and the whisper of a clue disappears.

"Hey, Eddie," I answer the phone and walk out of the office for privacy but not before I hear Tyler growl. If he's going to keep growling like that, I'll have to start buying him milk bones.

"Hey, Kristie," Eddie whispers.

"What's up?"

"I need to talk to you." The whisper now sounds a bit frantic.

"Okay, go ahead."

"No, in person." He pauses for a second. "I remember something about Dick. I don't know who else to tell."

"You called the right person," I assure him. "Where do you want to meet?"

"Can I come to you? Are you at the center?"

"I'm at my other job. Do you know *Callie's Cakes?*"

"I'll be there in fifteen minutes." He hangs up before I have a chance to warn him that he'll probably be facing a firing squad. I look up to see three males practically growling at me. Yep, an entire firing squad.

Chapter 21

Just pour the coffee straight in.

Eddie shows up exactly fifteen minutes later. Before I get a chance to even smile at him, Tyler grabs him and hauls him into the kitchen. He looks at me with confused eyes. I shrug and smile at him. My smile must not be very reassuring because now he looks scared, although that may have something to do with the big guys, Ben and Logan, standing in the kitchen waiting on the man and looking twenty different kinds of menacing. Do they practice looking scary in the mirror or something?

"What's going on?" His eyes glare at the men surrounding him, but his wobbly voice gives him away.

"Let him go, Tyler." I stare at him until he relents and releases Eddie. Eddie rubs his upper arm and glowers at Tyler. "Sorry about that. These guys are feeling a bit overprotective."

Eddie immediately switches gears. "Are you okay? Did something happen to you?"

I smile but shake my head no. "Not exactly." I clear my throat and hope I get away with the white lie. Compared to the other women in the forum, what happened to me was nothing. "Anyway, you said you remembered something about Dick."

He's not letting go that easily. "Are you sure you're okay? Why don't I give you a lift to the Youth Center and we can talk there?"

Bless his heart. He thinks I'm in danger and is trying to get me out of here. I genuinely smile at him now. I was totally right to hire him at the center. Time for some introductions. "This is Detective Evers and Detective Allen." The men grunt in recognition at Eddie. "You remember Tyler." I don't add that he has decided to become my shadow. Tyler walks over to me and squeezes my neck with his big hand before leaning down and kissing my forehead. "Her man," he fills in before tucking me into his side for protection. As if.

Eddie looks around with wide eyes. "What's going on?"

Ben and Logan give me looks of warning, but I pretend not to see them. "It turns out Dick was murdered."

"Murdered," he gulps just loud enough for me to hear it above the snarls coming from the men. They obviously didn't want me to reveal that information. Like I care. I trust Eddie and he's totally proven his worth today. "I thought he overdosed and was found in the alley behind the bar?"

Ah, so that's where everyone thinks he was discovered. I don't know who started the rumor that the guy was found in an alley, but I'll be sending them a fruit basket for Christmas. "Not exactly." I may be willing to reveal the murder, but if everyone thinks Dick was found in an alley, who am I to dispute that?

Logan's had enough. "You said you have some information about Dick?"

Eddie's eyes widen as he takes in Logan. The man has his I'm-scary-and-I-know-it-look going on. Eddie's eyes flare slightly in fear before his back stiffens. Good for him. He turns back to me to answer. "Yeah, um, I'm not sure if it's important or anything, but Dick was acting different before he … um… died."

"Different how?"

"Dick was a bit of a slacker. He wasn't a big partier or anything, just lazy and liked to goof off. He loved to play practical jokes, but they were all pretty childish. Anyway, a couple of weeks ago, he started bragging about his grades. He usually managed to carry a B- average by the skin of his pants, but all of a sudden, he was claiming he was going to get straight A's. The strange thing was, he wasn't studying hard. He was actually goofing off even more. I didn't even think that was possible."

"Did he say why his grades were improving?" Luckily, the men are allowing me to ask the questions as Eddie seems to have no problems telling me what he knows.

He shakes his head. "Nah. I asked, but he'd just laugh and say 'that's for me to know and you to never find out'. Whatever that meant."

"What did you think he was up to?" I ask because I have no idea what could possibly be the reason for Dick's grades improving.

"I figured he was having an affair with one of his professors." A cute little blush has formed on Eddie's face. Judging by the heat on my cheeks, he's not the only one sporting a blush.

Ben and Logan have had enough, which becomes apparent when they approach Eddie. "We're going to need you to come into the station and make a statement."

Eddie turns to me with wide eyes. "It's okay. You can trust these guys. They're the good ones." Even if they look scary as all get out at times. He nods at me before turning to follow the detectives out of the kitchen.

Tyler's phone beeps as soon as the door swings shut. He looks at it before cursing. "I've gotta go, baby," he whispers before kissing my forehead and following the men.

I turn to Callie and Anna. They're literally vibrating with excitement. Anna's bouncing up and down while Callie is smiling and rubbing her hands. She claps her hands before declaring: "Okay, let's get started."

"Started with what?" I obviously missed something.

"First, we need to find out who Dick's professors were. We need to see who the lady professors are. Oh, shoot, they're mostly women at your college, aren't they?" She practically runs into her office and plops down behind her desk before grabbing her laptop.

"How are we going to find out what classes Dick had?"

Callie stops. "Don't you have access to his schedule?"

I scrunch my nose up at her. "Why would I?"

"Isn't there anyone you can ask? What about that advisor dude? Timothy or something?"

"Mr. Timmer?"

She snaps her fingers. "That's it. Just ask him. I'm sure he'll give you the list." I'm not so sure about that.

"Wait!" Anna's shouts interrupt my protests. Is she going to be the voice of reason? "We don't actually know Dick had an affair. That's only what Eddie thought was going on. There could be a zillion other reasons Dick's grades were going to improve."

"Like what?" I ask because I seriously have no clue.

Anna shrugs. "Cheating is the first thing that comes to mind. You hear about test answers being stolen all the time."

I shake my head. "Nope. Dick was a junior. He shouldn't have any classes with simple multiple choice questions anymore."

"But if he had the essay questions, even if he didn't have an answer key, he could prepare his answers in advance and improve his grades vastly that way," Callie pipes in.

Darn it, she's right. "But how are we going to figure out if he'd gotten his hands on the tests?"

"We can search his dorm room." She's not only bouncing on her toes anymore, she's practically jumping up and down.

"I'm not searching his dorm room!" And knowing Anna, it'd be up to me to do it since I'm the student amongst this threesome.

"No one's searching his dorm room." I nearly fall off my chair with relief with Callie's return to sanity. "They've already cleared it out so that option's out." Back to insanity, it is. "Which leads us right back to where we started: the professors."

I have a bad feeling about this. "So you're going to talk to them? Professor to professor?"

Callie laughs. "Um, no. You'll be the one to do that."

"Wouldn't they be more likely to talk to you?" I'm getting desperate now.

She ignores my question. "I really think a student murdered on campus deserves some kind of memorial in the college newspaper."

Anna picks up the thread. "Definitely. He should be honored."

I am so not getting out of this.

Chapter 22

Procaffeinating: to delay or postpose actions; put off doing something until you've had your coffee.

To my surprise, Tyler doesn't make it back to *Callie's Cakes* before closing. He doesn't totally leave me alone, though. He texts me to tell me to 'be careful' and make sure the security guard at the Youth Center walks me to the car. Yeah, right. My car is parked six feet from the side entrance. The time at the center flies by. Although I haven't missed a shift at the place, by the amount of work I need to catch up on, I've clearly been neglecting my duties. That happens when you're busy trying to find a killer or a rapist. Or is it both? I decide to spend an extra hour or two catching up on paperwork. My phone dings as I'm closing down my computer.

Tyler: *Where are you!?!?!*

Me: *The Youth Center*

Tyler: *Why are you still there? Isn't your shift over?*

Me: *Needed to get caught up. Leaving now*

Tyler: *OK. Message me when you arrive @home & I'll escort you into the house*

Me: *Overprotective is a word. Look it up*

Tyler: *Don't care. Your safety is important*

Me: *Even if you make me mad it seems*

Tyler: *Yep. See you soon baby*

Which reminds me. We need to talk about him calling himself my man today. This whole calling me baby and thinking I'm his to protect is getting out of hand. But how am I going to bring it up with the man? I can't exactly walk up to him and say 'I'm not your baby; you're not my man.' Well, I could. If I were anyone else but Kristie, I'd probably not even have a heart attack doing it.

I park my car on the street in front of my apartment. I'm still debating whether to text Tyler or not when my door is wrenched open. "Hey, baby," Tyler says and bends over to kiss me. It's just a quick kiss, so why does my heart speed up? "How was your day?" He grabs my hand and pulls me out of the car before reaching over and grabbing my bag.

What was I thinking about on the way home again? Oh, yeah, how to tell Tyler we're not together. Doing a bang-up job with that so far, aren't I? We're in my apartment before I can get my brain to re-engage. "We need to talk," I finally manage to get out.

Tyler chuckles and pulls me to the sofa. "What do you want to talk about?"

I glare at him. "When a woman says 'we need to talk', you should be scared. Very scared."

He just smiles at me. I'm sure he's making the dimples come out on purpose. "I'm not going to let you run away from me, so go ahead, talk. I'll listen, but I'm not going to follow whatever bull you come up with to push me away."

My mouth drops open and I just stare at him. He chuckles again and now I'm mad. I shut my mouth and glare at him. I try to push his arms off me as well, but the guy has muscles of steel. "You can't have a relationship that's only one-sided! I get to choose as well!"

The smile finally drops from his face and he sighs. "I know, baby. But I also know you're pushing me away because you're scared. I don't know if you're scared because of what happened or if it's something else. I intend to find out." Uh oh. That doesn't bode well for me. "In the meantime, I'm not letting you push me away." He grabs my hand and holds it over his heart. "I know you feel this connection between us. A girl like you wouldn't put up with me being in her place and let me put my hands on you if you didn't feel something for me."

Darn. He's got me there. "I…" I don't get a chance to respond. He puts a finger over my lips to silence me.

"I know you're scared, baby. That's okay. We'll go slow. But I absolutely cannot let you push me away."

"Slow is good." I'm surprised I manage to speak at all. And where in the world did those words come from? That's not what I meant to say. I think.

Tyler smiles before leaning over and crushing his lips to mine. Oh my. This may be why I'm not pushing him away. He has magical lips. That must be it.

One of the advantages of being more fluent in the college intranet now is being able to look up Timmer's schedule. After we got disturbed at the Youth Center, we never got back to scheduling an appointment to discuss my last semester class choices. I quickly make an appointment for next week. Now he can't turn my dropping by to get Dick's schedule into an impromptu counseling session.

I quickly find a time of the day when he has back-to-back student meetings. I'll just drop by between the meetings and then he won't have enough time to quiz me on how well I'm doing. The memory of my college advisor seeing me at the hospital makes me squirm. And not in a good way. Once again, romance novels have let me down as none of my professors are swoon-worthy.

A student is just exiting Timmer's office when I turn the corner. I check my watch. Five minutes until his next appointment. Excellent. "Hey, Mr. Timmer," I shout as I knock on his open door.

"Kristie." He smiles as he stands and walks around his desk. "I didn't know we were meeting today." He leans on the edge of his desk; the picture of a man with all the time in the world.

"We're not." There's a flash of irritation on

Timmer's face but it's gone so quickly I may have imagined it. I quickly backpedal. "I mean. I couldn't get an appointment with you until next week."

His smile is back. "Ah. What can I do for you in the meantime?"

"Well..." I stutter.

He stands. "Are you doing okay? Feeling okay?" Shoot! I shouldn't have hesitated. The whole idea was to get in and out quickly thus preventing any interrogation – no matter how well-intentioned such interrogation may be.

"I'm fine. I just need some help."

"Of course. Whatever you need." He looks entirely too happy to help me.

"I'm working on a memorial for Dick Reynolds for the newspaper." I pause, but Timmer doesn't say anything. He just looks at me with a blank face. "I wanted to talk to some of his professors. See if maybe they have some funny stories or something I can add to the story."

Timmer finally speaks after an entirely too long and uncomfortable pause. "I'm not sure what you need me for."

"I was wondering if you had his latest class schedule. That way I can talk to the professors who have had him in class most recently."

He stares at me and I squirm under his scrutiny. Finally, he stands and walks around his desk to his computer. "I guess that won't do any harm." Luckily, it doesn't take more than a minute or two for the printer to start spitting out paper. He grabs the paper and hands it to me. "If that will be all?"

I smile and hope it doesn't look entirely fake. "Thanks. I'll see you next week."

"Indeed."

I rush out of the room. I'm sure it looks like I'm fleeing but at this point, because that's exactly what it is.

Chapter 23

Any friend of coffee is a friend of mine.

I decide to 'interview' Professor James first. I remember Dick's friend, Kevin, mentioning that Dick somehow managed to get her to sit on a whoopee cushion in his Intro to Social Policy class. Maybe her anger at Dick was really a ruse to keep their relationship secret. Listen to me – using words like ruse. I need to watch it before I follow in Lucy and Ethel's footsteps and start saying words like sitrep and run around thinking I'm some super private investigator solving crimes.

Intro to Social Policy is just getting out when I arrive. I wait for the students to file out before slipping into the classroom. I take one look at Professor James and nearly walk right back out. There's no way Dick was sleeping with this woman. I'd bet my last cup of coffee on it. With her grey hair and horn-rimmed glasses, the woman looks more like a grandmother than a professor. She should be home knitting booties for her grandchildren and not standing in front of a classroom. But we don't actually know that Dick was having an affair. We only know that he was bragging about his grades improving.

I take a deep breath and walk to the front of the classroom. Professor James turns to me with a smile on her face. I tower over the woman. She must be about Anna's size. I look down her old-fashioned pants suit and see the heels she's wearing. Nope, at least several inches shorter than Anna's midget height of five-feet.

"Hi." Wow. That sounded dumb. I clear my throat and try again. "I'm Kristie Larson." I reach out a hand to shake hers.

She shakes my hand before asking, "What can I do for you?"

"I'm working on an article about Dick Reynolds. A sort of memorial." I let the lie sit there, but James doesn't take the bait. "I'm talking to all his professors, trying to get a feel for him as a student. Maybe get some nice anecdotes to add to the article."

Professor James snorts. "Sorry, that was unprofessional of me." She shakes her head before continuing. "I've been teaching a long time." I don't doubt that. "I've seen a lot of kids walk through these hallways. Most of them are still kids struggling to become adults. Dick was a kid who didn't want to become an adult. He was childish. Frankly, I'm not even sure he would have passed this class."

Yet, Dick was bragging he was going to get straight A's this semester. Something fishy was going on, that's for sure. But was it something that could have gotten the man killed? I shake those thoughts out of my head and smile at the professor. "Well, thanks for your honesty." She nods and walks away.

One professor down. Two to go. Luckily for me, Dick was slacking off and only taking three classes this semester. I rush through the hallways, hoping to catch Professor McDonald before she starts her lecture on Contemporary Issues in Social Welfare. The woman is just coming out of her office as I arrive.

Now this woman I can see Dick wanting to have a relationship with. She's dressed like a rock star in black skinny jeans and a t-shirt with a V-neck just on this side of acceptable. On her feet are knee-high boots with a spike heel. No idea how she manages to walk in those things in the Wisconsin winter. Her jet-black hair shines above her crystal blue eyes. No wonder it's nearly impossible to get into her classes.

"Professor McDonald?"

She stops at my shout and raises an eyebrow at

me. "Yes?"

"Hi, I'm Kristie Larson. I'm in the master's program." I don't know why I said that. The woman's beauty is intimidating.

McDonald smiles. "Yes, I remember you. What can I do for you?"

I actually blush at the notion that this goddess remembers me. "Um, I'm doing a piece in *The Daily Cardinal* about Dick Reynolds. I believe he's in your class or was in your class." She nods but remains quiet. "I was wondering if you could tell me anything about him. Maybe an anecdote I can include in my article?"

She throws her head back and laughs. "I don't think anything I have to say about Dick could be added to your story as an anecdote."

Now, this is intriguing. "Really?" I struggle to keep my eyebrows from raising. "What do you mean?"

"Walk with me," she demands as she strides down the hallway. Good thing I have long legs to keep up with her. "Dick was... how shall I say this?... enamored with me." She chuckles. "The boy was always coming to my office on some pretense or other. I'm not stupid. Of course, I knew he was trying to figure out some way to get me into bed."

I nearly choke on my tongue but manage to squeak out my question. "And? Did it work?"

She laughs again. "Um, no. My wife would not have been too happy with me cheating on her with a student of all things." She shivers. "And a man." She shakes her head. "Um, no. I haven't experimented with boys since I was in college myself."

I can't help it. I giggle at her obvious revulsion at sleeping with the male of our species. But something else she said has got my ears perking up. "You said he was in your office all the time. Is there any way he could have gotten his hands on the final exam?"

She stops and turns to me. "Hmmm... there's something going on here that the infamous college rumor mill has not heard about." I sputter, trying to come up with a way to keep this conversation from being added to that very same rumor mill. "Don't worry. Your secret is safe with me." She continues walking. "Anyway, there's no way Dick could get his hands on my exam. I don't write the exam until the last moment so I can concentrate on areas students are struggling with. And I always do that at home."

We arrive at her classroom and she turns to me and smiles. Oh, yeah, I totally get why Dick was obsessed with this beauty. "If there's nothing else?" She doesn't wait for my response but opens the door, leaving me in the hallway. I can't help but watch the sway of her hips as she saunters to the front of the classroom.

I shake my head and rush off. I need to get to class as well. I'll have to do my third 'interview' later.

⁂

I'm walking out of my Social Work and Adolescents class when I nearly run into the very professor I need to talk to. "Professor Linn," I say in surprise.

"Yes?" she responds with a smile. Linn was always one of my favorite professors. I'm really hoping she's not involved with Dick in some way. Although I have a hard time imagining the tiny Asian woman having an affair with a twenty-year-old goofball, I can't simply eliminate her because of my personal feelings.

"Do you have a moment?"

She nods in response and we move out of the sea of students rushing from classrooms. "I'm doing an article on Dick Reynolds." The lie is getting easier with each repetition. "He was a student in your Poverty and Social Welfare class."

"Yes," she sighs. "I remember Dick. He's the student that died of an overdose, isn't he?"

I nod. "I'm trying to write a sort of memorial article about him so that he isn't remembered as that kid that

OD'ed."

"Huh." She doesn't say anything for a moment. Should I prod her again? "I'm not sure there's a good way to remember Dick."

Well, that's not what I expected her to say. She always seemed like such a kind teacher to me. "What do you mean?"

"I'm sorry," she says with a shake of her head. "But the boy was completely lazy. He always showed up late to class. His assignments were never on time. And then there were the stupid practical jokes. A whoopee cushion is funny once. Maybe. Not every single class. Frankly, I'm not sure if he would have passed my class this semester."

Gosh, darn it! Another professor who, without any prompting on my part, is convinced that Dick was failing. How in the world did he think he was going to pull off straight A's? I shake my head before smiling at Professor Linn. "Well, thanks for taking the time to talk to me."

"I hope you find what you're looking for," she says before turning and walking away.

Huh? It almost sounds like she knows I'm not actually writing an article. Guess I'm not the stellar liar I thought I was.

Chapter 24

Coffee! You can sleep when you're dead!

The doorbell rings before I've had time to warm up from the cold commute home from the Youth Center. Before I can even think about answering, Tyler shouts: "I've got it." The man has sure made himself at home in my apartment. I turn at his chuckle. "Lucy and Ethel are here."

Normally, I get a break from the dynamic duo in the evenings as they get up early to do the baking at *Callie's Cakes* before I arrive to open the place up. Well, Anna does the baking. I'm sure Callie thinks she helps. More likely she drives Anna crazy by quoting inane trivia about the chemistry of baking or something.

"How did it go today?" Callie is still in the hallway and shouting to make herself heard.

I ignore her question. "Good evening to you, too. Coffee?" I don't bother waiting for a response and turn to start making the liquid of the gods.

Anna bounces to my tiny kitchen while rubbing her hands. "Yes, something warm would be lovely."

I probably shouldn't give the bouncing pixie coffee after 9 p.m. but soon she'll be Logan's problem and not mine. Apparently, I have a vicious streak because I giggle at the thought of the big guy dealing with an out-of-control pink-haired pixie. I've always thought Anna and Logan were a bit of a mismatched couple, but maybe scary Logan is the one to tame rambunctious Anna.

"You got any beer?" Speak of the scary dude and

he shall appear.

Tyler pulls three beers out of the refrigerator. Guess Ben is here as well. I take my time with the coffee. There's no rush. None at all. I didn't find anything out from Dick's professors after all. I hand coffees to the girls before making my way to my living room, which seems even smaller with three over-sized alpha men occupying it. I sit on the armchair while Tyler sits on the armrest. Ben and Logan pull their women onto their laps. I have no idea if Callie or Anna want to sit on top of their men. It's not like they get a choice in the matter.

"So, what did you find out?" Callie's done being patient.

"Nothing."

Anna snorts. "I sincerely doubt that."

I roll my eyes at the pink-haired pixie. She just wants to start trouble. "Seriously, there wasn't anything to learn. At least not about why Dick thought he was going to get straight A's. All of his professors thought he was an immature goof-off who would barely make it through the semester."

"So why did he think he was doing well?" Callie taps her fingers on her chin. I call it her 'thinking-mode'. "Maybe he did steal the exams?"

I shake my head. "Nope. At least not all of them. Professor McDonald said she writes the exam at home. There's no way Dick could have gotten his hands on it."

"Okay. I'm lost!" Anna throws her hands in the air. "I don't get how dead guy could have thought his grades were improving. He wasn't schlepping any of his professors and it looks like he didn't get his hands on the exams."

"No idea." I sigh and collapse against the back of the armchair. Tyler reaches out and squeezes my shoulder. "Dick was such a goofball. There's no way he could have pulled off anything stealthy like drugging women and taking them back to their college dorms without getting caught or at least bragging about it."

"And we still have no clue why anyone would want him dead." *Thanks for the reminder, Callie.* Fortunately, my snarky inner thought doesn't manifest itself in my voice.

That tickle of a clue is starting to form in my head. *Drugging woman. Taking them back to their dorm rooms.* "Hold up!" I raise my hand and, surprisingly, everyone quiets down. "There's something we're missing. Something super important and obvious." The picture finally forms and I snap my fingers. "Coffee stains! How did we miss that?"

"Miss what?"

"Okay, think about it. Where were all the women when they discovered what had happened to them?"

Callie doesn't miss a beat. "Naked in bed."

"Whose bed?"

My boss smiles and bows her head to me. "Good thinking, batgirl."

"Good thinking? What thinking? And who's batgirl? I thought I was batgirl."

Logan hugs the bouncing girl sitting on his lap. "Want to share with the rest of the class?"

I can't help the smile that covers my face. I can't believe I thought of something the two super detectives didn't. "Each of the assaulted women woke up in their own beds – in their dorm room." I look around but besides Callie, no one has filled in the dots. I decide to give them another clue. "Who can get into a dorm?"

"Alex was in an all-female dorm." Tyler jumps up and starts pacing. "Are you telling me that this... this rapist ... has a female accomplice?"

I jump up and grab his hand to stop his pacing. "No. I'm telling you that whoever has been drugging and assaulting these girls has to have access to the dorms. Who has access to the dorms?"

"I do." At her proclamation, everyone turns to Callie.

"You think we're looking for a professor." Ben studies me, obviously surprised I figured out a clue they missed. To be fair, the men have been out of college for more than a decade.

Callie responds by pulling out her trusty notebook. "So," she says as she flips through the pages. "We're looking for someone who has been with the university for at least four years and has access to the dorms. Other professional staff, besides the professors and lecturers, have access to the dorms as well."

Tyler sits in the armchair and settles me on his lap. "Did you do background checks on any staff?"

Logan and Ben shake their heads, but I answer on their behalf. "There's no need. Everyone in the School of Social Work has to have a background check." When everyone just stares at my announcement, I shrug. "You can't exactly be a social worker with a criminal background."

"The staff as well?" Ben pulls out a notebook and starts making notes.

"I assume so. Anyone who wants to keep their accreditation would have to maintain a clean record."

Ben looks at Logan who nods in response to some silent question before standing with Anna in his arms. He kisses her before announcing, "We're going to go look into those background checks."

"Make sure you check into the staff as well." Callie can't help but give them further instructions. "They aren't studying to be social workers. They wouldn't have had background checks."

"Are you concentrating on the School of Social Work?" Tyler asks as he follows the men to the door.

"To start, yeah." Ben answers before he and Logan head out. Tyler shuts the door behind them.

"So, what do we do in the meantime?" Tyler groans at Anna's question.

Callie shuts her notebook. "Let's let the men do

their background checks. I'll find out from Ben if there's anything interesting to follow up on." Thankfully she doesn't expand on how she's going to wheedle the information out of the man. "In the meantime, I need to get some shut eye."

I turn around after locking up, after Callie and Anna leave, to discover Tyler standing right behind me. "I thought they'd never leave." He doesn't give me a chance to respond before his lips descend on mine. Not that I'm complaining, mind you.

Chapter 25

Give me coffee and no one gets hurt.

A week has passed while Callie and Anna's men do deep background checks on anyone with access to the women's dorms who is associated with the School of Social Work. The troublesome twosome is actually quiet, content to wait on the checks to be completed. They make me nervous when they're not plotting destruction.

Tyler, however, has not been letting any grass grow under his feet. Although he had to go back to work, he managed to finagle his way into training courses all week so he could still stay with me instead of at the firehouse during his shifts.

Push. Push. Push. That's Tyler for you. He's still insisting he's my man and – whenever I protest – he kisses me silly. I thought the whole 'kiss me silly' thing was another romance book lie. Nope. Sigh.

My mind is still on Tyler and his scorching kisses as I walk into school. I've put it off long enough and now I have no choice but to not only make an appointment with my advisor, Mr. Timmer, but I'm going to actually have to show up and stay this time. I wish he'd just ignore the fact that he saw me nearly naked in the emergency room. Avoidance! That's the adult way to handle things, isn't it?

My phone rings as I finish climbing the stairs to Timmer's office. I quickly grab it to see that it's Tyler calling. Since my procrastination has me running late, I hit *ignore* before silencing it and shoving the thing back into my pocket. Timmer's door is closed when I approach.

There's nothing for it. I take a deep breath and knock on the door. I nearly sob in relief when there's no answer. I struggle with turning around and heading home before forcing myself to knock a second time. Still no answer. Yes! I'm out of here.

Bang! I spin around and head back to my advisor's office. I'm sure that sound came from his office. I lean my ear against the door and listen. Sure enough, there's someone in there. I can hear drawers opening and closing as well as the squeak of a chair. I knock again. The noises immediately stop and I'm pretty sure I hear someone swear.

What do I do? I have no idea. I know what Anna would do in this situation. She'd barge in first and think about it later. No help there. But what about my super nerd boss, Callie? What would she do? She'd probably barge in as well. Why don't I have any wimpy friends, darn it!

I grab the handle and push the door open before I can talk myself out of it. "Mr. Timmer." My voice falters when I take in his office. It's a complete and utter mess. "What's going on?"

My advisor finally looks up from where he's shoving files into a briefcase. I register surprise in his eyes before his eyes narrow. He places the case on the ground and shuts the drawer before standing up. "Shut the door, Kristie."

His words sound like a demand rather than a request. A shiver runs down my spine and I know I'm in trouble. There's no way I'm shutting that door. I slowly inch my way backwards toward the hallway. "What's going on, Mr. Timmer?"

He laughs, but he's obviously not amused. "Oh, now you want to take the time to talk to me after running away from me for weeks?"

"I was embarrassed! You saw me in a see-through gown at the hospital for coffee's sake!" Even thinking about it weeks later, I can feel my cheeks heating up.

He throws his head back and laughs. It sounds

almost like a cackle. Can men cackle? "And all this time, no one even thought to wonder why I was there?"

His words stop my retreat. "What in the name of day old coffee are you talking about?"

His eyebrow raises and he just stares at me. My mind is a total blank. I have no idea what he's hinting at. When I refuse to say anything further, he shakes his head at me in what looks like disappointment. Why in the world would he be disappointed in me? I'm more confused than ever. "Blondes," he mutters with another shake of his head.

I start to defend my hair color when he speaks again. "No one on this campus has a clue about what happened to you." Where is he going with this? "Yet, there I was only minutes after you arrived at the hospital. I just happened to be 'passing by'."

When he pauses, waiting for my response, I just mutter, "That's what you said."

He laughs again. "Just how in the world did you get this far in life." He snaps his fingers. "Oh, that's right. You have a rich mommy and daddy to take care of you."

"Hey!" That's totally not fair. I've worked hard to get where I am. Harder because mommy and daddy didn't approve.

Timmer moves around his desk and stalks to me. He grabs my elbow and pushes me against the wall before I even register he's touching me. I lift my hands and push against his chest, but he's not moving. He sneers down at me. "You ruined everything!" I open my mouth to respond. Before I manage to utter a sound, Timmer's speaking again. "I had a good thing going here. A good job with excellent benefits." He winks at me and licks his lips.

"Oh. My. God." It finally all clicks together for me. "It's you. You're the one hurting the students."

He lifts a hand and grabs a strand of my hair. When I try to move away, he pulls hard on my hair. "Hurting? I'm not hurting them. They're so drugged out of their minds, they don't even know what happened the next day."

"And that makes it okay?" My anger must give me additional strength because this time when I push him away he actually moves. "Just because they don't remember being abused by you doesn't make it right!"

"Of course, you would think that. You're so naïve and innocent even I couldn't get over that and enjoy myself with you."

"You drugged me!" I'm not sure he can understand my words with how loud I'm screaming. "You killed Dick!"

He sneers. "Killed is such a nasty word. It was an accident."

Something snaps in me. I rush at him and use the only weapon I have. I run my fingernails down his face. Obviously, I'm not a fighter and have no idea what I'm doing. I hear shouting, but I can't comprehend any words through the haze of my anger. Who knew that you do indeed see red when mad enough?

Suddenly, something or someone is pulling me away from Mr. Timmer. I'm not happy about that at all. "Let me go!" I wrestle with the force. "I'm going to kill him!"

"Shh...." Someone whispers into my ear. "I've got you. It's me. Tyler." He continues to whisper nonsensical whatnots into my ear. I manage to calm down enough to see that the office is now flooded with police. Ben and Logan are cuffing Timmer while uniformed officers rifle through the drawers and papers strewn about the room.

"What's going on?" I throw the question out there for anyone to answer. No one responds.

"Get her out of here," Logan demands and I remember why I find him super scary. The look on his face is enough to make me think I'm going to pee my pants. Good thing Tyler's pulling me away before my bladder has a chance to embarrass me.

Tyler doesn't say a word as he escorts me back to my apartment. He holds me tight and nearly drags me along. My anger gradually fades as we walk. By the time we make it back to my place, I just want to lay down and forget this semester ever happened. The troublesome twosome is waiting at my door. Looks like that nap's not happening anytime soon.

"Is she okay?" I must look pretty out of it if Callie is asking about my well-being instead of what's happening with Mr. Timmer.

Tyler doesn't answer. He unlocks the door and pushes me inside. After everyone follows him in, he locks the door and grabs my hand again. He sits in the armchair and pulls me onto his lap. "Are you okay?"

I shrug. "I'm not really sure what's going on."

"What happened?" Anna's done waiting for an explanation.

Instead of waiting for her to pester me into submission, I answer. "I had an appointment with Mr. Timmer today. I need his approval on my class selection for next semester." I shake completely inappropriate thoughts of how I need to find a new advisor out of my head before continuing. "He didn't answer when I knocked and I was ready to take off when I heard a crash. I listened and I could hear drawers opening and closing so I knew he was there. I knocked again and went in. He was packing up everything. It didn't really register what was going on." I swallow the lump that has appeared in my throat before gathering the courage to continue. "He admitted to drugging the women and killing Dick."

I feel the long stream of breath Tyler lets out. He must be relieved that the man who hurt his sister will finally be punished for his crimes. I squeeze his arm that's banded around my waist. He kisses my neck and I cuddle into him.

"Good thing Ben did those background checks."

"What are you talking about?"

"Turns out your advisor didn't have a nervous breakdown like you thought. He got fired after several allegations that he was abusing the teenage girls in his charge."

"Seriously!" I try to jump out of Tyler's lap, but he's

Self-Serve Murder

holding me too tight. "Why isn't he in jail?"

"He quit before the investigation was finished and took off."

"And no one from the college called for a reference?" I can't believe it! All this pain and suffering could have been prevented if someone had just checked his references.

Callie shrugs. "I don't know. I'm sure they'll be looking into things now."

"Too late," I mutter.

Tyler hugs me close and shushes me. "It's over, baby. You're safe. Let's concentrate on the positive right now."

I shake my head, unwilling to let things go. "What about Dick? Why did he kill him?"

"The boys think it's blackmail." I just stare at Callie until she continues. "They found a bunch of 'I know what you did' emails from Dick to Timmer."

"And Dick thought Timmer would up his grades?" Idiot, I think but don't say. Never speak ill of the dead and all that.

Callie and Anna stand. "We just wanted to check to make sure she was okay. Take care of her for us."

"I always will."

Always? What?

Epilogue

Love is in the air and it smells like coffee!

I snuggle into the warmth of my bed. I have absolutely no desire to get out from underneath these covers and go try to save the world today. I wiggle into a more comfortable position. Wait a minute! Those aren't covers I'm wiggling against. Oh, god. I've seen this movie. I didn't like the story – at all.

"I can hear you thinking," Tyler whispers into my ear and all of a sudden, I understand the concept of sexy morning voice.

My body immediately relaxes at the sound of his voice. No creepy naked guys here. My mind, however, is a completely different matter.

"Relax. I know you're innocent and we need to go slow with the physical stuff."

"What?" Tyler keeps talking over my admittedly lame attempt at a question.

"Shush, baby. I don't care. I can do slow. Doesn't change the fact that you're my woman."

There he goes again with the 'you're my woman hear me roar' speech. I don't care that Callie and Anna positively melt over that kind of talk. It's not my thing. "I belong to no one!"

He chuckles and I'm pretty sure mutters 'stubborn' under his breath. He pulls gently on my shoulder until I'm lying flat on my back. Leaning over so his face is directly over me, he responds, "Don't you get it?" I don't respond. My brain may have short-circuited when he leaned over me. "If you're my woman, I'm your man."

Oh, well that does make things sound a whole lot better. He plops down on his back next to me and my brain goes back online. "Why?" I croak and clear my throat before continuing. "Why are you still here? I'm safe. You can go home now."

"Baby." Suddenly, he's looming over me again and my brain struggles to pay attention while my eyes can't help but wander down his chest. He's not wearing a shirt! "After what went down yesterday, I couldn't stand to be away from you." I don't respond. My eyes are entirely too busy checking out his abs. So, that's what they mean with a six-pack!

At Tyler's chuckle, I tell my wandering eyes to stop it this minute! "So what happens now?" Yep, I'm that lame. I have no idea how to have a relationship.

"We date, which I imagine will result in me spending a whole lot of time at *Callie's Cakes* since my girl works entirely too much."

"I can do that."

At Tyler's chuckle, I realize I said the words out loud. He's silently laughing as his lips descend on mine. Apparently, I'm more courageous than I thought because I reach a hand out and begin to explore those muscles exposed by Tyler's shirtless state. I may have been missing out with the whole no-time-to-date thing. Tyler tilts his head and deepens the kiss. No time like the present to start making up for lost time.

Grasshopper Cake Recipe

This cake is a pain in the butt to make, but it's absolutely fabulous to eat! I finally managed to find this recipe hidden in one of my boxes, which had been stored in a container in Germany for the past two plus years. After I managed to get rid of the horrible musty smell on my books, I re-discovered this recipe. I'm totally obsessed with mint combined with chocolate. Unfortunately, that appears to be a very American flavor combo as I can hardly find it anywhere. Dr. Oetker to the rescue!

For the Cake

100 grams butter

200 grams white flour

20 grams cocoa powder

3 teaspoons German baking powder ('Backin')

125 grams sugar

1 package vanilla sugar

4 medium-sized eggs

100 milliliter milk

For the Filling

2 sheets white gelatin

300 grams whipping cream

30 grams sugar

150 grams After Eight

For the Icing

4 sheets white gelatin

125 milliliter peppermint liquor

30 grams sugar

300 grams whipped cream

50 grams After Eight

Instructions

1. Pre-heat the oven to 180 degrees Celsius.

2. **For the cake:** Melt the butter and leave to cool. Combine the flour, cocoa and backing powder in a mixing bowl. Add the remaining ingredients and use a hand mixer to mix. Start slow and gradually increase to a high speed for approximately 2 minutes. Should make a smooth batter. Place the batter in a greased spring form pan (approximately 26 centimeters in diameter) and flatten. Bake for approximately 25 minutes in the pre-heated oven.

3. Remove the cake from the pan and place on a wire rack to cool. After cooled, divide the cake into two pieces. (I bought a special wire thingy to do this because me and knives do not get along.)

4. **For the filling**: Place the gelatin in cold water, following the package directions. Place the gelatin in a small bowl and stir slowly until completely dissolved (do not cook the gelatin). Let slightly cool. Beat the whipped cream with sugar until nearly stiff. Add the lukewarm gelatin and beat until stiff. Chop the After Eight and add to mix.

5. Place the bottom cake on a cake platter. Spread the filling over the cake and add the cake top.

6. **For the icing:** Dissolve the gelatin as described under point 4. Stir in the liquor and sugar with the gelatin. Beat the whipped cream until stiff. Fill a piping bag with a star spout with approximately 2 tablespoons of the whipped cream. Add the remaining whipped cream to the liquor mix. Frost the cake top and

sides with the mixture. Use the piping bag to decorate the top of the cake. Use the After Eights to finish the decoration. Place the cake in the refrigerator for two hours before serving.

About the Author

D.E. Haggerty is an American who has spent the majority of her adult life abroad. She has lived in Istanbul, various places throughout Germany, and currently finds herself in The Hague. She has been a military policewoman, a lawyer, a B&B owner/operator and now a writer.

Printed in Poland
by Amazon Fulfillment
Poland Sp. z o.o., Wrocław